JUHANI AHO (1861-1921) was born Johannes Brofeldt on Sept. 11, 1861 in the village of Lapinlahti, eastern Finland. Aho's first collection of short stories, or *lastuja* ("wood shavings"), as he called them, was published in 1883, and his breakthrough masterpiece, *The Railroad*, appeared the next year. *The Clergyman's Daughter* (1885) and *The Clergyman's Wife* (1893) address the position of a passionate female protagonist suffering in the roles afforded her in old Finland. In *To Helsinki* (1889), a young student experiences the freedom of life in the city. Aho's *Alone* (1890) draws on his experiences in Paris and shocked readers with a description of a visit to a prostitute. Of his later work, *Juha* (1911), an intense novel of adultery and suicide set on the eastern frontier of Finland, was the most successful. It has been adapted for film four times. Aho had three children, two by his wife Venny and one by her sister, Matilda. He died in Helsinki on August 8, 1921.

OWEN WITESMAN holds an MA in Finnish and Estonian area studies from Indiana University. His translations include Petri Tamminen's *Hiding Places* (Aspasia), Anita Konkka's *A Fool's Paradise* (Dalkey Archive), Kari Hotakainen's *The Human Part* (MacLehose) and several forthcoming crime novels and thrillers. Owen also has translation credits in nonfiction, children's literature, poetry, comics, and graphic novels.

Some other books from Norvik Press

Kjell Askildsen: *A Sudden Liberating Thought* (translated by Sverre Lyngstad)

Victoria Benedictsson: *Money* (translated by Sarah Death)

Hjalmar Bergman: *Memoirs of a Dead Man* (translated by Neil Smith)

Jens Bjørneboe: *Moment of Freedom* (translated by Esther Greenleaf Mürer)

Jens Bjørneboe: *Powderhouse* (translated by Esther Greenleaf Mürer)

Jens Bjørneboe: *The Silence* (translated by Esther Greenleaf Mürer)

Johan Borgen: *The Scapegoat* (translated by Elizabeth Rokkan)

Kerstin Ekman: *Witches' Rings* (translated by Linda Schenck)

Kerstin Ekman: *The Spring* (translated by Linda Schenck)

Kerstin Ekman: *The Angel House* (translated by Sarah Death)

Kerstin Ekman: *City of Light* (translated by Linda Schenck)

Arne Garborg: *Tha Making of Daniel Braut* (translated by Marie Wells)

Svava Jakobsdóttir, *Gunnlöth's Tale* (translated by Oliver Watts)

P. C. Jersild: *A Living Soul* (translated by Rika Lesser)

Selma Lagerlöf: *Lord Arne's Silver* (translated by Sarah Death)

Selma Lagerlöf: *The Löwensköld Ring* (translated by Linda Schenck)

Selma Lagerlöf: *The Phantom Carriage* (translated by Peter Graves)

Jonas Lie: *The Family at Gilje* (translated by Marie Wells)

Viivi Luik: *The Beauty of History* (translated by Hildi Hawkins)

Henry Parland: *To Pieces* (translated by Dinah Cannell)

Amalie Skram: *Lucie* (translated by Katherine Hanson and Judith Messick)

Amalie and Erik Skram: *Caught in the Enchanter's Net: Selected Letters* (edited and translated by Janet Garton)

August Strindberg: *Tschandala* (translated by Peter Graves)

August Strindberg: *The Red Room* (translated by Peter Graves)

Hjalmar Söderberg: *Martin Birck's Youth* (translated by Tom Ellett)

Hjalmar Söderberg: *Selected Stories* (translated by Carl Lofmark)

Anton Tammsaare: *The Misadventures of the New Satan* (translated by Olga Shartze and Christopher Moseley)

Elin Wägner: *Penwoman* (translated by Sarah Death)

THE RAILROAD

OR, A TALE OF AN OLD MAN AND AN OLD WOMAN WHO HAD NEVER SEEN IT BEFORE

by

Juhani Aho

Translated from the Finnish by
Owen Witesman

With original illustrations by
Eero Järnefelt

With an introduction by
Jyrki Nummi

Norvik Press
2012

Originally published in Finnish by Werner Söderström under the title of *Rautatie* (1884).

This translation © Owen Witesman 2012
This introduction © Jyrki Nummi 2012
The translator's moral right to be identified as the translator of the work has been asserted.

Norvik Press Series B: English Translations of Scandinavian Literature, no. 53
No. 1 in the series: Classics of Finnish Literature.

A catalogue record for this book is available from the British Library.

ISBN: 978-1-870041-89-8

Norvik Press gratefully acknowledges the generous support of FILI, Finnish Literature Exchange, towards the publication of this translation.

This book contains 17 illustrations by Eero Järnefelt, first published by Werner Söderström (now WSOY) in 1892. The illustrations were digitized from the original version by Tatu-Pekka Kekäläinen.

Norvik Press
Department of Scandinavian Studies
University College London
Gower Street
London WC1E 6BT
United Kingdom
Website: www.norvikpress.com
E-mail address: norvik.press@ucl.ac.uk

Managing editors: Sarah Death, Helena Forsås-Scott, Janet Garton, C. Claire Thomson.

Cover illustration: Illustration by Eero Järnefelt.
Layout: Elettra Carbone
Cover design: Elettra Carbone
Printed in the UK by Lightning Source UK Ltd.

Contents

INTRODUCTION

The Vanishing Idyll in Juhani Aho's *The Railroad*

> Our artists ought to find poetry in the stations
> as their fathers found it in the forest and fields. –
> Emile Zola (1877)

The Railroad is a comic novel on the impact of modern times in the rural areas of Eastern Finland. The first railway in Finland was built between Helsinki and Hämeenlinna, opening to the public a year after Aho's birth in 1861. In 1884, when this novel was published, the Savo railway did not yet exist; the railway to Kuopio was only built in the 1890s, extending to smaller regions such as Lapinlahti and Iisalmi as late as the beginning of the next century. It was not by chance that Aho incorporated modern technological innovations into his early stories: the electric lamp, the clock (watch) and the railway. Just like the Parisian impressionist painters Manet and Monet, and the naturalist writers Zola and Maupassant, he was fascinated by this new mode of transport that forced the world to move ever faster and connected people together, and that people largely welcomed the industrial and technological revolution.

The title of *The Railroad* may be read as a simple reference to the contemporary world on its way towards modern society. In this fictional tale Aho brought the modern world and its technological infrastructure to Finland, the remotest corner of Europe, making the outside world suddenly appear not so far away after all. Indeed, the subtitle suggests an unexpected connection. The story is 'the tale of an old man and an old woman who had never seen it before'.

Matti and Liisa are a childless couple who live by themselves in an isolated house as tenants of the parsonage. When they hear that a new railway has been built in the village of Lapinlahti, they spend the winter and spring thinking about it, and finally decide to take the long walk to the village on Midsummer's Day. The railway station, with all the new people, important officers and Swedish-speaking ladies from the city, the train and, finally, the unsuccessful trip on the train, are too big a slice of life for Matti and Liisa to cope with. Their 'expedition' results in great disappointment.

This simple-looking story is one the best-selling books in Finland, not least because of its long-standing popularity in the school curriculum. It articulates the most significant signs of change in the final decades of the nineteenth century. The first edition, however, sold slowly; the book was reprinted in 1892 with illustrations by Eero Järnefelt, a well-known painter and member of the famous Järnefelt family. On the maternal side the Järnefelts had their roots in the St Petersburg aristocracy. Elisabeth Järnefelt established an important literary salon and an influential critical circle for the young writers of the 1880s. As part of the 'Järnefelt school', as the circle was called, the young Aho became acquainted with new trends in Russian and Scandinavian literature, and this led him to steer modern Finnish literature towards more European models.

The shift in Finnish literature from Romanticism and Idealism to Realism and Naturalism took place almost imperceptibly through the course of the 1880s. The short stories of the 1870s, dealing largely with the spread of civilisation to the lives of common rural people in the forests, obscured the special nature of Finnish realism. There was also a fundamental change in the idea of what 'real life' truly was, as dominant idealistic aesthetics gradually disintegrated under the pressures of modernity.

Why did the author attach such a formulaic subtitle to a simple, matter-of-fact title and realistic story? In a letter to Elisabeth Järnefelt, Aho gave readers a clue when he explained the need for the addition: 'I think that it might be slightly more comical if I do not simply leave the name Railroad there by itself, but somehow [the subtitle and] the whole story will assume a somewhat lighter, humorous form'.

The 'lighter, humorous form' refers to the general character of the story. But it is also an ironic indication of a stylistic twist in the long expository part of the novel. Through the window of his study, the pastor sits following little incidents in the yard. Then he notices Matti and remarks that he is very short. He concludes that his size must be linked to the fact that Matti has no children (the narrator makes the parenthetical observation that the pastor himself has seven children). There then follows a summary of the simple lives of Matti and Liisa:

> And so it was: children Matti had none. A wife he had, Liisa, but no other household at all. Together they lived, two alone, in the small cottage of Korventausta in the parsonage forest tract. Old they were both – and so they had been for many years now – and small. Small was the horse as well, a nag mare, though strong, and small was also Liisa's cow. Of the outside world they knew little and the world knew of them less still. A few times they visited the land of men each year – for church at Christmas three Sundays in a row, at Midsummer, and for confession on Good Friday.

The language of this short passage is typical of contemporary fairytales for children. Every sentence begins with an adverb or even a predicative. This is not neutral syntactic word order in Finnish. In abundant use, it easily creates the impression of infantile language, a sort of baby-talk. Aho used the 'inversion style' in other stories too, in an attempt to achieve specific artistic design in his prose.

The later proponents of 'pure language', the modernist generation of the 1950s, considered inverted language a grave stylistic fault. However, they failed to see the specific function of this device. As we can see in *The Railroad*, the narrator replaces neutral representation with this particular stylistic formulation for a restricted passage in which he gives a description of this couple. Immediately after the passage above, sentence structures revert to the neutral mode. What is the meaning of this little passage, which has gone completely unnoticed in the criticism of Aho's novel? It offers a minor, yet important clue as to how we might appreciate this homely old couple. At the same time it represents a part of the larger changes that the Finnish novel underwent in the 1880s.

The narrative innovations of *The Railroad* caused embarrassment and confusion amongst critics at the time. A well-known review by Julius Krohn made the point. The reviewer was appalled at how the story 'dives into details' and 'forgets' to narrate – so much so that 'the whole idea' of the novel disappears. Description, in the manner of Zola and Maupassant, had entered the novel. Narration had been relegated to the background; dialogue and description now took centre stage. The shift changed rhetorical norms: detail, abundant wording and slow pacing replaced economy, clarity and linearity.

The Railroad begins with a broad *tableau* depicting a Finnish winter morning. The sun shines, bathing the church and the bell tower in a golden glow. The first paragraph is a sign of the changed status of description in narrative prose:

> The frigid cold forces its way into every corner, streaming over the ridges of the fence and winnowing rime ice into the trees and bushes. The sun gilds the crosses of the church and bell tower, shining cheerfully into the frosty birch grove and illuminating every column of smoke pouring in curls from chimneys and smoke holes near and far. The road is not quite screaming for dear life under the runners of the sleigh, although it groans sorrowfully, forlornly.

The picture of the wintery landscape of Finland, so natural to a modern reader, was something quite new to the contemporary reading public. This little nature sketch is designed like a 'still life' and seems to belong more to the art of painting than to the art of narrative.

Then the narrator shifts his attention to a magpie sitting in a fir tree in the garden. As the magpie enters the tableau, the opening descriptive passage glides into this new scene in which the bird is given a central role:

> A magpie is perched in the topmost branches of a spruce tree, neck short and thick, head sunken into its feathers. At the break of day it set out from its night perch in the pine wood behind the field, flying behind the drying barn and over the cowshed before settling down in the parsonage garden, where a spruce stands all alone surrounded by birch trees.

The story then turns to a slow narration that functions as description in the service of exposition. After the expository part of the novel, the magpie suddenly reappears only to disappear once again. The bird follows the old couple, and his continuous laughter upsets Matti and Liisa. When the couple later return from their unsuccessful railway journey, the magpie is waiting for them, sitting in a tree by the road, and begins to call and jeer at them again.

In folklore the magpie is known for its curiosity and babbling – a metaphor for the narrator. The cry of the magpie is also common in folklore, where it is seen as a sign of good news or of a welcome guest. Its jeering laughter anticipates a pleasant guest for the clergyman, but for Matti the bird's shrill tone ironically anticipates 'good news' – that is, the news of the railway. The magpie is a *personnage-introducteur* who introduces the reader to the scenery and characters of the novel from an unexpected angle. Later on, the bird acts almost as a formal character who appears to follow the events of the story and reacts to them with his nasty cackling. The use of such a fable-like external focaliser represents a fundamental transformation from a simple tale to an artistically oriented narrative. The bird opens up new formal possibilities, announces several motifs and creates within the novel a playful atmosphere.

The elements of rustic humour and the narrator's psychological observations have both been emphasised in later criticism of *The Railroad*. As much as Matti and Liisa are 'genuine' rural Finns, they are also local characters, representatives of the Savo people. They are old and small; indeed, they have been old 'for many years now' as the story begins. They have little to do with the outside world; they live their lives in their far-away house, and only once or twice a year do they go to church or to the parsonage. These people are original and simple; they are wary of everything new and unknown.

When dealing with other people, Matti is careful to ensure that his ignorance does not show. He feels immediately insulted if he notices that someone is trying to fool him. He is eager to show his physical strength – which he naïvely takes as a measure of his manhood. Liisa is certainly not the weaker vessel in this marriage, though her ignorance is no less than her husband's. She is curious, cunning and more socially sensitive than her husband. She is also quick to make observations on human relations, attitudes and differences of opinion.

That being said, the couple is not presented satirically. The portrait of Matti is heightened as he – in contrast with those social contacts outside the home circle – becomes more self-assured and his new knowledge makes him proud and complacent towards his wife. Liisa, on the other hand, amuses herself all spring by keeping a piece of information to herself and not revealing it to her husband.

The Railroad is also a comedy of marriage. The balance between husband and wife is maintained by the act of communicating – or not communicating. The way the couple remains silent is characteristic of people living in the woods. Closing one's mind and remaining silent is natural in the middle of such vast forests. The human mind is connected to the cycles of nature; as winter approaches, the mind becomes silent until the spring sun reawakens it and people once again begin to open their souls and mouths. Matti and Liisa are deeply connected to their environment, to nature, and this reveals the cultural level on which life is lived in Korventausta.

Later criticism has considered *The Railroad* the story of a larger cultural vision. The theme of the novel was established early on as the transition from the past to modern times, even as a collision between the modern world and the original, idyllic state of nature. The key word was 'idyll' and it has remained in our critical vocabulary ever since.

The latter half of the nineteenth century saw the publication of a vast body of literature on distant cultures and peoples. The traditions of the Fenno-Ugric peoples drew particular interest among enlightened readers in Finland. Aho, for instance, was fascinated by *The Voyage of the Vega around Asia and Europe*, an extensive report on the fragmented Arctic peoples and their lives, published in 1881 by A. E. Nordenskiöld.

Critics from Viljo Tarkiainen to Juhani Niemi have described Matti and Liisa as representatives of 'primitive people'. They contend that the couple are presented in their most natural element, in the middle of the Arctic darkness, the snow and the cold. Matti has never used a rifle in hunting – he uses traps instead – and he never forgets to cast spells as he sets them. As he returns from the parsonage, the railway begins to bother him. Travelling through the winter twilight into the depths of the forest Matti looks at the cold winter sky with its falling stars and wonders whether the invention of the railway will provoke any heavenly sanctions.

The connection of the primitive people to the distant couple from Korventausta is clear enough, but the link itself is quite general. The couple's connections to Finnish literature are more specific. First of all, 'Matti' has a special status as a representative of the typical Finnish man and, more generally, of all Finnish people in nineteenth-century literature. He appears in Topelius's *Maamme kirja* ('The Book of Our Land', 1875) where his fate is to pick stones out of the fields. In Runeberg's *Tales of Ensign Stål* (1848–60) Matti serves as a faithful farmhand, and in the epic poem *Deer Hunters* (1832) as a poor crofter. Pietari Päivärinta, a contemporary of Aho, published the short story 'Puutteen Matti' ('Matti of Scarcity', ca 1880s) about a poor common man living in the woods who travels to town in order to pay his debt to a greedy pastor. This Matti dies on the trip and his family's meagre possessions are sold off at auction. The narrative is sentimental in tone, and the moral lesson is strongly emphasised.

In Aho's story Matti is again used to describe the ordinary Finn who has momentarily left his mundane existence to face the modern world. In Topelius's story 'Aunt Mirabeau', a long passage is devoted to a description of the first railway trip from Helsinki to Hämeenlinna. Topelius employs the metaphor of 'Matti the Finn' to describe the astonishment of the ordinary Finnish man, who could not stop wondering at the speeding ghost of modern times.

> That March 17th was a remarkable day, a giant step for Matti the Finn into the twilight air of the future. How amazed Matti was that day! First the flags were fluttering everywhere, then the cries of hurray were heard all around, then the new monsters came roaring through the loneliness of the forests – and with that the first railway between Helsinki and Hämeenlinna was opened!

All these literary roots suggest that the nature of Matti and Liisa is not primarily an anthropological one. Instead, their story may be read as a commentary on the changing role of the Finnish people in literature.

Another literary connection runs through 'the primitive dimension' – the small-scale lives of Matti and Liisa, a feature remarked upon by all critics – but not in the genre of anthropology. Everything in the story associated with Matti and Liisa is depicted on a miniature scale. Matti is short and Liisa is short; their house is small, as are their horse, their cows, their fields – everything that surrounds them is small. The same applies to their activities, their thoughts and their feelings. There are no grand vistas, no depths nor heights; there are no great passions, no emotions. Their conversation is trivial, their admiration and hate is petty; their quarrels are mild. Every human trait seems to be small, without any sign of growth. What is the meaning of this smallness? I do not think it is primitiveness.

Matti and Liisa represent a variation on the Dantean theme of *limbus infantes* (the area in Hell where innocent children were placed after death), a subject Kivi also treats in his narrative poem *Lintukotolaiset*. 'Lintukotolaiset' is part of ancient Finnish mythology as recorded in Christian Ganander's book *Mythologia Fennica* (1703), where Kivi originally became acquainted with it. *Lintukoto* ('the home of the birds') is populated by miniature human-like beings that were called *lintukotolaiset* or *taivaanääreläiset* ('inhabitants at the edge of heaven'). Equivalent beings are to be found in the cultures of other ancient peoples and in the mythologies of the Arctic peoples. *Lintukoto*, a mythological place, is typically situated in the Far South or the Far East, at the edge of the world or at the point where the sky meets the earth. Everything was small there, perhaps due to the proximity of the sky or the lack of space. Migratory birds flocked there in the winter and a human soul could move there after death.

Matti and Liisa are not primitive in any anthropological sense used in Aho's day or subsequently. They are certainly not 'brutes', though they are not noble – regardless of how that word might be applied to savages or the poor. Their backwardness and 'smallness' is of a specifically literary nature.

The most characteristic trait of daily life in Korventausta is repetition and monotony, notions that are highlighted in several ways. Everyday duties become identical, almost ritualised activities. Visits to the outside world are repetitive, as are, for instance, Matti and Liisa's regular topics of conversation and Matti's obligatory drink with the pastor. Repetition reveals much about the couple's world view. Matti and Liisa do not think that anything could ever change in the world.

Repetition is a mark of the idyllic genre, as Mikail Bakhtin outlines in his study on novelistic chronotopes. It is a world that is spatially small, limited and sufficient unto itself, not linked in any intrinsic way to other places or with the rest of the world. Everything happens there twice, thrice, an infinite number of times. Everything proceeds in cycles. The influence of the idyll on the modern novel has proceeded in several directions. In a Finnish context the influence of the idyll on the 'provincial' novel – a very popular genre across mid-nineteenth-century Europe – was of great significance. The provincial novel was an important genre in the early development of the Finnish novel and related shorter narratives often called 'village stories'. The provincial novel generally concentrates on issues of family, labour, agriculture or handicrafts. All temporal boundaries are blurred and the rhythm of human life is in perfect harmony with the rhythm of nature. Common everyday life is transformed: the events of everyday life take on a special significance, and the cyclical repetition of life processes is of crucial importance. The same heroes as in the idyll – peasants, craftsmen, rural clergy, rural schoolteachers – populate the provincial novel just as they do *The Railroad*.

The protagonists from Korventausta live the happy idyll even though everything around their time-vacuum has fundamentally changed and will eventually be replaced. The passing of time does not yet affect them. There are no worries, no sickness, not even a shadow of death in this world. Life in Korventausta is a painless and effortless existence. Although Matti and Liisa must be quite old, they do not seem to be affected by age; for instance, they do not mind walking long distances. They may tire, but there is no suggestion that this might be due to their age. Their lack of children has roots in the idyllic world: it is a world of eternal being, where there is no growth and there are no children. It is an eternally infantile world with no sexuality, no problems, no birth, and no death.

The destruction of the idyll (understood in its widest sense) was to become one of the fundamental themes in Finnish literature towards the end of the nineteenth and into the first half of the twentieth centuries. In Russian literature – and, consequently, in Finnish prose literature written under the era of Russian influence – the chronological boundaries of this movement shift to the second half of the nineteenth century. The destruction of the idyll has been treated in a multitude of ways in European literature. The destructive force was met violently in the French realistic novels of Flaubert and Zola; in the Russian novel, the theme received somewhat softer treatment, as in the classic case of Goncharov's *Oblomov*.

In far-away Korventausta the railway – first as a thought and an indefinite image, then as the decision to go and have a look at it – breaks the idyll, breaks the cycles and the repetition. Matti and Liisa leave their home and set off on a long journey. The reader understands that, when the couple return home after their frustrating trip, a change will have taken place, something that will steer their world in a very different direction from before – though Matti and Liisa will perhaps never know anything about it.

Professor Jyrki Nummi
University of Helsinki

I.

*T*he frigid cold forces its way into every corner, streaming over the ridges of the fence and winnowing rime ice into the trees and bushes. The sun gilds the crosses of the church and bell tower, shining cheerfully into the frosty birch grove and illuminating every column of smoke pouring in curls from chimneys and smoke holes near and far. The road is not quite screaming for dear life under the runners of the sleigh, although it groans sorrowfully, forlornly.

A magpie is perched in the topmost branches of a spruce tree, neck short and thick, head sunken into its feathers. At daybreak it set out from its night perch in the pine forest beyond the field, flying behind the drying barn and over the cowshed before settling down in the parsonage garden, where a spruce stands alone surrounded by birch trees.

The magpie still has not received his breakfast. The kitchen door does not open, and no one is driving in the parsonage farmyard. Yesterday a kind maidservant tossed some scraps to the magpie, and yesterday as soon as one person left the main house with his horse, another would come...

Someone is driving up from behind the sacristy now, too – will he come here? No, he does not come into the yard; he turns out onto the ice, driving past below the parsonage, struggling to keep speed across the ice, the horse covered in hoarfrost, and the man's beard... The magpie's mood turns sad. It is hungry and cold. It does not even laugh at the pig now, its old friend, over there rooting at the door of the pigpen. Yesterday the magpie might have laughed at it, but now the bird cannot be bothered.

The magpie sinks even deeper into its feathers, not caring to pay attention to anything, to think anything.

So the magpie does not notice that a horseman is approaching across the ice from beyond the point. He climbs up the bank into the yard, stops his horse in front of the kitchen, pulls at the reins, drives forward a little more, and turns towards the birch tree that grows on the other side of the yard next to the gate.

'Whoa! whoa!'

Only now does the magpie notice him. He titters and bobs his tail; his heart leaps for joy, and he flies down to a post on the garden fence.

The man hitches his horse to the birch tree, sets a blanket on its back, pours oats into the feed bag, and adjusts the blanket one last time.

'That should hold now.'

When the magpie notices that the man has set off towards the kitchen, is already stamping his feet and preparing to enter, he moves to the uppermost branches of the birch tree next to the gate and peers down, his head cocked to one side. And when the man is out of sight, he descends to the lowest branch and begins to laugh – there is food for the taking, if only he dares. The magpie jumps to the ground; the horse lays its ears back, and the magpie laughs even more smugly.

The pastor is standing at the window of his chambers, blowing long puffs of smoke against the glass. He has been watching and waiting to see if the magpie would dare to snatch something. And as he waits, he smiles and pauses in his smoking.

'Ah, aha! And he's pinched it already ... now, what did he get ?'

'Would the pastor be so good as to take some coffee?' comes the voice of the maidservant behind him.

'Put it on the table there. Look – look! There he goes again, and now again – no, the mare won't give him any! Isn't that Matti Korventausta's* mare?'

'Must be, since Matti himself is in the kitchen ... he says he has business with the pastor.'

'Tell him to come here. What business is he about?'

'I didn't ask.'

'He's probably here making a grain payment, since there are sacks in the sleigh. Tell him to come through the front door.'

The pastor sits down in his rocking chair, puts his pipe upright on the floor against the table leg, and begins to drink his coffee. But every now and then he stretches back to see the magpie and Matti's horse.

'And now it doesn't dare try any more... .'

The magpie had flown to the roof of the granary after the horse had tried to kick it with its hind leg. Now it gazes down at the ground, mood downcast.

Matti is already stomping at the porch.

'Good day, Mr. Pastor!'

'Good day – and how are things with Matti?'

'The same as always ... and you, Mr. Pastor? The weather is a bit dry.'

'Twenty degrees below. Matti, sit, take the chair there.'

'Oh, I've had a good sit already. So, twenty below, eh?'

'Yesterday it was thirty.'

'Thirty...you don't say....'

'Have you come from home, Matti?'

'From home, yes. I'd like to make the grain payment on our lease, if the pastor can see clear to take it. I haven't had a chance to bring it any earlier, but yesterday Liisa said, "Now go tomorrow and take the lease grain – the pastor may think you aren't going to pay."'

'Oh, there is still plenty of time yet... .'

'If your man could come to take it, I could pull up right in front of the storehouse; then I can unbridle the mare to eat.'

'The inspector ought to be in the cottage. Come back here for some tobacco afterwards, Matti.'

When Matti had gone, the pastor leaned his chair back again so he could see from the window to the yard.

A pig had found the sleigh and was doing its best to rip a hole in the side of a sack. The blanket had fallen to the ground from off the horse's back – it had been found by another pig, which was rolling it in the snow. The magpie was jumping all around and clawing each pig's back in turn. The mare shook her bells and flattened her ears.

'Hey-ya! Pigs!' Matti roared as soon as he reached the steps. Snatching the broom handle that was lying in the yard, he rushed at the pigs. He managed to land a blow on the back of the one ripping at the sack. It squealed sharply and jumped away, knocking the other in the side. They ran together for a little way and then stopped to listen, heads together. But the magpie flew quickly to the other side of the farmyard. This was so amusing to the pastor that he could not help laughing out loud.

Matti ran into the cottage and then came back out with the foreman – whom everyone called the inspector because of his responsibility for lease payments –, and drove his horse to the front of the storehouse.* The pigs began to follow, but when Matti bellowed again angrily, they did not dare. But the magpie glided down from a spruce to where the sleigh had been and began his breakfast.

That old cuss still is awfully stout, even if he is small, mused the pastor to himself, when he saw Matti carrying a great sack from the sleigh to the storehouse. *I wouldn't be up to that, even though I am a younger man... .*

The pastor began to rock gently in his chair and blow smoke up towards the ceiling.

'But he just doesn't have any children... .' (The pastor already had seven of them.)

Smoke rings wandered towards the ceiling, expanding, rising higher, touching the ceiling, floating back down, disintegrating, and breaking into numerous smaller circles.

'...no children, even though he's been married longer than most. How long has it been now? How is it that some have them and some don't?'

And so it was: children Matti had none. A wife he had, Liisa, but no other household at all. Together they lived, two alone, in the small cottage of Korventausta in the parsonage forest tract. Old they were both – and so they had been for many years now – and small. Small was the horse as well, a nag mare, though strong, and small was also Liisa's cow. Of the outside world they knew little and the world knew of them less still. A few times they visited the land of men each year – for church at Christmas three Sundays in a row, at Midsummer, and for confession on Good Friday. At the end of January, then, it was customary for Matti to bring the lease grain to the pastor and trade spun yarn for fresh flax and wool with the pastor's wife for Liisa. Between these times, they passed their lives in the heart of the woods. In the spring, Matti felled a small plot of forest, burned it during the following summer, and sowed, tilling his patch of field and planting half in rye and half in potatoes. Then, during hay season, he and Liisa collected hay together for the horse and cow from the meadows and sides of the brooks. When autumn came, and for the winter months, Matti snared birds and hares; a gun Matti had never held. Liisa helped Matti with outdoor work in the summer, feeding the cow, the pig, and the cat in the winter, and then spun from Michaelmas to Whitsun wool and linen for the pastor's wife.

'You're still a stout fellow, Matti,' the foreman said when he came out of the storehouse with him, and Matti threw his nearly empty sack onto the sleigh.

Matti always liked it when people called him stout. But he still always exclaimed, 'What's that about me being stout? An old man like me ... It isn't right to poke fun at an old man – you're certainly stouter than me, Mr. Inspector.'

'I certainly am not. What are you on about? Saying your aren't stout when you can carry a two-bushel sack on your back!'*

'Oh, there wasn't more than a little over five pecks in that.'

'That's still something, that is.'

'I'm not much for strength any more, but it was different when I was a young man.' And, with eyes aglow, Matti told the same story he had told every time he made the grain payment. The story went like this: when he was still a farmhand at this same parsonage, he had once been threshing in the drying barn, and when it came time to carry the sacks from the barn to the storehouse, another farmhand – 'lazy lout that he was, even if he was big' – was not carrying his weight...just said that he was tired. 'It'll go just as easily without you, too, goddammit,' Matti had said, pulling a sack onto either shoulder and adding to the farmhand that, 'If you want, go ahead and jump on top yourself, and then you can have a free ride out to the yard!' Then the foreman had brought Matti a shot of liquor from the late pastor (the current one was the third to hold the position in Matti's memory).

'But what can I do any more, now that I'm an old man. I'm not like to be paid in shots any more.'

'And wasn't it then that Liisa took a fancy to you, Matti?' the foreman said, feigning ignorance.

'May have done. Hey now, girl!' Matti turned his horse towards the backyard. The foreman jumped onto the skis of the sleigh.

'It was after that when Liisa began to think "that's the one for me, that Matti" – don't I know it!'

The foreman brought this up because he knew that talking about it made Matti happy. Even though the foreman was a proud sort of man otherwise, now and then he liked to banter.

'Yes indeed, truth be told, it was after that when Liisa took a shine to me, even though she pretends not to even hear when you say it to her. "Don't you go on now; you've been a miserable slob your whole life!" she just says, even though she doesn't really think so.'

'Wasn't it Liisa herself who admitted it to you, Matti, that it was after that when she started to take a fancy to you?'

'How do you know so much about it, Mr. Inspector?'

'That's just what people say.'

'And you aren't just making it up, Mr. Inspector?'

'Not me – that's what I've heard Liisa say herself.'

'Liisa herself? She doesn't go so far as to say it, even though I still know that's how it went. She thought I was a slob before, but then she saw. As they say, even a short man has his feet on the ground.'

'Liisa was a stout girl herself before.'

'Weelll!' (Matti tore the horse collar's buckle open energetically.) 'She may be still. A normal healthy sort of person...'

Matti hitched his horse to the prow of the sleigh and looked at the foreman with a sly glance.

'And what of you, Mr. Inspector – how are things for you in that way? Liisa said that over Christmas she noticed that – '

'That what?'

'That you and the kitchen maid...' and Matti looked at the foreman even more slyly.

'Me? No! Old wives' tales! Go on and put a little more meal in the mash.'

'Oh, this is enough.'

The foreman decided to surprise Matti with a bit of news; that was really why he had started the conversation.

'You probably don't know that I'll be starting up as a station man soon.'

'Huh? As a what man?'

'A station man.'

'What kind of a man is that?'

'It's a kind of man that shows the way to guide them when they come to the station – a flag in the day and a lantern at night, white if it's clear to drive by, but red if they have to wait. It's a good position.'

To Matti it was a perfectly peculiar position. But he did not say so to the foreman.

'But why are you leaving this house, Mr. Inspector?' he asked instead.

'The pastor is related to the Lapinlahti inspector, and I'm going to live near the church in Lapinlahti.'

'And we don't need one of these...way-showers...in our own village?' Matti said.

'What would he do here, when the railroad is up there?'

'The *rail* road?'

'Yes, yes, the railroad. The iron road.'*

'The *iron* road?'

'The one that goes from Kajaani to Kuopio, and from there on to foreign parts, even to Helsinki, if you want.'

'On that road?'

'Yes, yes, you just sit in the carriage.'

'And that will get you to Helsinki?'

'In one go!'

'Don't you have to stop for feeding now and then?'

'No need – the railroad's horses eat while they run. Do you know what the railroad horses eat, Matti?'

'No, I don't.'

'They eat logs.'

'Now Mr. Inspector, I'm an old man, don't...logs while they run? I don't believe it.'

'It's logs they eat,' the foreman assured him.

But Matti always broke off all conversation when he realized his leg was being pulled. He pretended he could not even hear the foreman any more, just set his lips together and shoved the waiting mash in front of the groping mare.

The foreman did not see any point in trying to explain any more; he threw the bunch of keys over his shoulder and went, whistling, towards the cottage.

'Thought he could pull my leg – you were wrong, fool.'

Matti covered his horse carefully with the horse blanket and leathers and went to speak with the pastor.

'We measured out the grain – six pecks – enough for our small cottage,' Matti said when he had entered and sat down near the doorway on the chest in which the church records were carried to the yearly readings of the catechism.

'Matti, come in, come in. There are chairs about, too... .'

'I'm fine here.'

'Here's a pipe and the tobacco is over there.' The pastor

brought Matti a pipe and showed him where the tobacco box was on the edge of the tile stove.

Matti put some tobacco in the pipe, struck a match, and then put it out with his fingers...then carried it carefully to the stove. For a time Matti and the pastor sat without speaking. The pastor rocked in his chair, and Matti puffed little clouds of smoke from the bowl at the end of the pipe's long stem.

'Have you been able to keep healthy, Matti?' inquired the pastor.

'By the grace of God, yes, I've been healthy. This old age just sometimes tries to slow me down.'

'You aren't an old man yet, Matti – it takes a stout fellow to still be carrying a two-bushel sack on his back.'

'Where did you hear that, Mr. Pastor?'

'I saw it with my own eyes when you carried it on your back, like it was nothing.'

'Like it was nothing? Heh! heh! heh! So you saw that, did you?'

'Even though I'm younger, I wouldn't even be able to budge it.'

'Oh, I'm sure you would, Mr. Pastor... . I was able to when I was a young man, too.' And Matti told the pastor that when he was a farmhand, here at this same parsonage, during the time of the previous pastor, once he had been threshing straw and when it was time to carry the sack from the barn to the storehouse, this one farmhand – 'lazy lout that he was, even if he was big' – did not offer to carry his part...said he wasn't able. But then Matti pulled two sacks onto his back and said to the other farmhand, 'If you want, jump on top yourself as well, and you can have a free ride to the yard.' Then the foreman had gone and talked to the pastor, and a little later he had come out and said that the pastor had ordered him to give Matti a drink for the good work.

Matti glanced under his eyebrows at the pastor. The pastor rattled the keys in his pocket, stood up, paced the room a couple of times, pulled his hand and a key from his pocket and went to his cabinet. He opened it – as he had every time before when Matti had visited and told this tale – took out a bottle and a tumbler and told Matti to come and take a drink. Matti objected as he had objected each time before – saying that it might go to the head of such an old man – but then took a shot nonetheless, as he always had before. The pastor put the bottle and tumbler out of sight again, locked the cabinet, slipped the keys into his pocket, and sat down to rock.

They talked about this and that, falling silent now and then and smoking.

Then the pastor's wife came in as well to shake Matti's hand and chat. She asked what was new and how Liisa was feeling.

'Nothing in particular. Liisa is feeling quite well – we can't complain as long as there is bread on the table and wood in the stove...'

'You should bring Liisa to church more often, Matti. You don't bring her to church more than a time or two each winter,' the pastor's wife said.

'I'm sure it's never only been once – she could come two or three times, if she wanted.'

'Doesn't she want to?'

'No, she doesn't really, now that she's got glasses so she can see well enough to look at the Book herself.'

'Do you still see well without glasses, Matti?'

'Me? – No, ma'am, I haven't been able to see for a long time – blind as a stump; I can't see anything no matter how I try.'

'You should get glasses, Matti.'

'Glasses? – No ... I've tried them, but they don't suit me.'

Matti did not dare look at the pastor. The pastor rocked and puffed smoke at the ceiling. He glanced at Matti – he knew that Matti was a poor reader, a very poor reader.*

'Who would feed the animals if Liisa was going to church every Sunday,' Matti said.

'You should take a maidservant to help Liisa; you are a wealthy man, Matti.'

'A wealthy man, me? Certainly not, ma'am – just so long as there's bread...'

'A man who is said to even have money out on loan...'

29

'The world is full of rumours – it's just good that we have food on the table.'

'In any case, at least you should take Liisa to see the railroad, Matti. I don't suppose you have been there yet yourself?'

'Nooo, I haven't. Is it very far?'

'It isn't far from here. When we left after breakfast, we were at the railroad by midday. *Huru långt ä' de' nu heller, pappa, ti' järnvägen?*'*

'You know the Lapinlahti church, of course, Matti?' the pastor asked.

'Yes, I know of it, even though I haven't been there.'

'The railroad goes by right near Lapinlahti church.'

'So that's where it goes, eh?'

'If you set off one morning, by the next morning you're in Helsinki.'

'That quick, eh? Does it take long to go to foreign parts? I hear you can go there as well.'

'It depends where you go – you can get to France in five days if you travel hard.'

'And to America?'

'You can't get there by railroad, since there is the ocean in between. Look here, Matti. Here on the map you can see there is this sort of wide sea between, the Atlantic Ocean.'

'So it seems.'

'But it does go fast, and it's very different to travel in than clattering along in our carts.'

'I should think so.'

'It doesn't jolt – and it goes so fast that it blurs your eyes.'

'I should imagine it does. Is it the crown** that put it up?'

'The crown, indeed.'

'The crown is always up to things like that. I should imagine that it gets along at a good clip if the crown puts his stallions in front of it. But I was still wondering ... is it really true how they say that the railroad's horses eat logs. It probably isn't; was the inspector just poking fun at me?'

The pastor and his wife, though they were learned folk themselves, still never laughed even if they thought someone happened to say the most foolish thing. And how would Matti have known? Where would he have found out? And when the pastor's wife really thought about it, horses were the thing that had come to mind for her in the beginning as well when she first heard talk of the railroad; even she had thought: *a* rail *road*? Of course it would be a road made of rails like a boardwalk is made of boards or a dirt road is made of dirt and mud. Sometimes people even called it the 'iron road.'*

The pastor had already been a university student when he saw the Helsinki railroad for the first time and did not remember any more what he had first thought it would be like. His mouth began to form a laugh, but then he started to explain, quietly and patiently.

'It's like this, see, it doesn't need horses – the carriages move by steam power. You've seen carriages, of course?'

'Of course I've seen carriages before!'

'They aren't the same as we have; they have to be different, the ones that go by steam power.'

'Of course they have to be different.'

'They're like rooms almost.'

'Ah, like rooms – you don't say!'

'And they're propelled by steam like steamboats ... you've seen the *Suomela*, haven't you, Matti?'

'I did see it last summer chugging along in the bay there near the church.'

'Well now, that is propelled through the water by steam, and the locomotive, that is, the engine that pulls the carriages, it is also propelled by steam. Instead of paddles it just has wheels because it moves on the ground.'

'Yes of course – it couldn't use its paddles to move across the ground.'

Yes, now Matti understood perfectly what it was like – it was a thing like a steamboat but lifted onto wheels. Still, it was a bit of a strange setup... . But of course the pastor knew well enough, since he'd seen it himself.

'Do you understand now, Matti?'

'Now I do, now I do!'

'Yes, that is what it is like,' said the pastor's wife. 'Matti, take some coffee ... and bread as well. You should go and see it and

take Liisa along.'

Matti drank his coffee but did not respond.

'I imagine I should believe it even without seeing. Why should an old man care any more about all these amusements? I know what it's like, now that the pastor has explained it.'

'No one can explain it perfectly to someone else,' the pastor's wife said. 'You have to see it with your own eyes. Indeed, you must go and see it!'

'Thank you, thank you! So I really ought to go?'

'Yes ... yes, indeed; and take Liisa along.'

'It may well put her in a mind to go, when she hears of it.'

The pastor's wife went about her business, but the pastor and Matti still chatted about this and that. They chatted about how much the human intellect thought and invented and where it would go yet.

And the pastor said, 'Just so long as it doesn't reach beyond its strength and run out of control.'

'And start acting up,' Matti said.

'It is certainly good for man to use his intellect, which was given him in the Creation – if only he doesn't turn to pride and forget the Giver of all,' the pastor said and added, 'They are the works of God as well, these steam engines and railroads.'

'They certainly aren't anyone else's,' Matti agreed.

And he marvelled greatly at this strange contraption that was like a room lifted up on wheels... But the pastor had begun to yawn and his speech begun to falter ... and so Matti made his goodbyes and left.

II.

*M*atti was rather absent-minded as he harnessed his horse and did not remember to put the bit in his horse's mouth until he had driven across the yard. He only noticed his mistake once he was in front of the kitchen. The mare was not in any hurry either as she walked across the yard and then on down the bank to the ice.

But Matti was in no mood for her impudence.

'Ho, mare! What's going on there! Hup-hup-hup!'

But the mare was waiting for a better curse than that. Pretending not to hear, she just dragged her feet as she did when pulling a water barrel.

'Hup-hup-hup!... ain't you up to it?' Matti jerked the reins, first right, then left, and this let the mare know he meant it now. Before she really broke into a trot, she whisked her tail, twice, because that was her way, you see. Then she leapt into a trot, since on the downhill the sleigh was coming hard behind.

The magpie was sitting on the top bar of a fence. It hopped from there onto a post and let out a smug laugh.' That bird is sure having a good time... laughing at nothing,' Matti muttered and snapped the reins to get his mare into a better run. '... don't you understand that even the magpies are laughing at you!'

The mare trotted rhythmically across the ice, which creaked under the runners of the sleigh, which rattled as it went. Matti sat rigid in the middle of the sleigh with the collar of his fur coat turned up. The short day was already drawing towards darkness. Matti drove along, following the road markers, and

thought...
Matti thought about his conversation with the pastor and his

wife. So there was a railroad at the Lapinlahti church? He would
not have believed it if he had not heard it with his own ears ...
and it was strange indeed that he had not heard of it before ...
it must have just arrived there... Wasn't the steamboat content
with the water? Why did it have to climb up onto dry land? It
must surely be a strange sight – it was already strange enough
chugging across the water ... should he go and take a look –
had others gone besides the pastor and his wife?

The road markers made a bend at the head of the peninsula

and then curved across the lake to the base of Talvilahti Bay, to the shore by the Huttula house. The closer they came to land, the more leisurely the mare jerked along. Matti had not hurried anywhere in a long time, and the mare thought she could go ahead and walk. Her hind legs were still running although the front ones were already slowing to a walk. And then the rear ones were walking and her croup heaved as if sighing in relief.

'Hup-hup-hup!' The mare had to start running again with its front legs; the hind legs were still walking. But when Matti jerked the reins, first right, then left, the hind legs were obliged to fall in with the rhythm.

Matti always had a habit of watering his horse at the head of Talvilahti Bay at the hole kept in the ice at the Huttula house. And from old memory, the mare veered that way now as well.

'Hup-hup-hup!' Matti would not have remembered now, but the mare was insistent.

'Oh, go on then!' Matti said, giving the mare the reins.

At the break in the ice the waterman from the Huttula house was filling a tub.

'Where are you coming from, Matti?' the waterman asked.

'From the church... . I was just at the parsonage,' Matti answered, climbing out of the sleigh to knock the snow from his mare's hooves.

'Any news over there?'

'Nothing in particular. Is the master of the house about?'

'No... left this morning for Lapinlahti.'

'He must be off to see the railroad.'

'Sure, but he's already seen it before. More like he's off to buy something.'

'The master's trading has been going well?'

'All right, I imagine. I don't know – at least he looks to be fattening up.'

'Have you been to see the railroad, Ville?'

'Who, me? I was there building it with my own two hands.'

'Hold on now... .'

'No, really – a year and a half it was, and I'll be off again soon as well.'

'What sort of work was it?'

'Just like digging ditches.'

But Matti did not believe that. He pursed his lips together and said nothing. He did know a little, enough that he could not be made a fool of so easily. He knew enough about the railroad and such things that he knew building them was not digging ditches. Stinking old Ville might know how to dig a ditch, but build a railroad? No one but a smith would be able to do that.

'Have you been to see the railroad, Matti?'

'May have done.'

'How did it look?'

'How did it look? You should know best yourself.'

Ville had already filled his tub with water and offered the bucket to Matti. Matti pulled water from the opening in the ice and let his mare drink.

'You're a stout man, Matti, lifting a full water bucket with one hand,' Ville said.

Matti did not say anything to that, but still he felt appeased.

'Have you ever ridden the railroad?' Ville asked again.

'Have you?'

'Of course, and how! It goes so fast the best stallion wouldn't be able to keep up if they raced.'

'It could if you let it gallop... .'

'It might in the beginning, if you let it gallop,' Ville admitted.

Matti scooped up another bucket of water for his mare, this time with his left hand.

'The inspector from the parsonage is going to the railroad too towards spring,' Ville said.

'He seems to be saying so... whether he actually will or not.'

'We're going together – the inspector is going to be a station man, but I'm headed for other work.'

'What work?'

'Rail maintenance. We're leaving as soon as spring comes. I've been lodging here at Huttula doing this and that, but as soon as the ground thaws I'm off to repair the railroad. Without repairs it can't run.'

'But iron would last . . .'

'That's exactly what doesn't last. The rails are always getting loose, so there always have to be repair men. Come along and work there too, Matti!'

'Nah, I'm not about to work for the crown.'

'Not even if the crown pays a good wage?'

'How much do they pay there?'

'Two marks a day.'

'Like during the best hay time?'

'Exactly, just like that. Come along and work for the crown, Matti!'

'That I won't do.'

'It ain't no different from any other work – you'd be able to do it for sure.'

'Sure I'd be able to do it just like anyone else. I just don't care to.'

'The missus probably wouldn't let you go!'

'The missus? Forget my wife!'

'Isn't your old lady a bit strict?'

'I know my wife well enough. Here's your bucket, here!' Matti answered, a bit resentful of Ville's presumptions. He sat down in his sleigh and started to drive away without saying goodbye. The Huttula waterman raised the bucket to his tub and started climbing up from the bank of the waterway.

Matti drove towards the end of Talvilahti Bay, picking his way along using the road markers. He climbed back onto land at the fishing net drying shed and after traversing a forest road for a short distance came to the main road, which looped around the lake and met up here with the shortcut.

Maybe I'll have to make a visit, thought Matti, who was not able to think of much else but what he had heard. A railroad... although he could not quite make out what it was, no matter how hard he thought and guessed. And still Matti could not help but think about it, but as he thought he was again in danger of getting tangled up. Each time he imagined it, it looked different. Now and then he would be on the verge of figuring it out, but then it would change again. First it was as if there were before his eyes a four-wheeled wagon with wheels both large and small, always wanting to look like the ones on the dead pastor's old carriage. And in front of the carriage there seemed to be two horses, with the pastor sitting with his wife under the hood, and opposite them, the young gentleman and ladies; in the coachman's seat sat the driver, hands outstretched, and, next to the driver, Matti, as a small boy, a little afraid and holding on tight. Then sometimes there were no horses and no carriage and no nothing, until he started imagining the *Suomela*, as if it were traveling along the road on wheels, large and small, a flag affixed to a pole on the prow, and the captain standing stock still astern. Behind, on a line, came two, no three flat bottom boats. And as they went downhill they knocked up against each other, and the men could not seem to get them separated. And the clatter and knocking was like the whole congregation from church driving along together.

For Matti all of this felt like something from a dream. Although it had to be like that, since even the pastor had seen it and explained it so. And of course they had made it, the people who built it, so that it would work well and there would not be any trouble on the downhills or the uphills either. But how? – that Matti was not able to explain to himself. And what was it needed for anyway? And so for a long time Matti ignored any thought of the entire thing. He flicked the reins to set his mare to trotting, dug out some fresh pipe ash from his pouch and stuffed it in his cheek.

But then as the mare ran she took mouthfuls of snow from the side of the road, and Matti wondered if she were thirsty even though she had been able to drink at the hole in the ice at the Huttula house. And without realizing it, Matti's thoughts stole from the hole in the ice to the bucket, from the bucket to Ville, and from Ville to the railroad... . The man had *ridden* the railroad... . How many times?

And since it had not been explained in any detail, how did it move and how did you drive it and what was it like? Did it have big wheels and small wheels like a carriage, or were they the same size, or what? But in any case, it went fast, since the best trotting horses could not keep up! But how could that be? Was it an exaggeration that not even the best trotter... ?

That was too much, blast it, too much bragging! If a strong man in a cutter sleigh were to really soften up the sides of a good trotter with a sharp whip, and if the road were as smooth as iron and there weren't any bumps and there was good weather, then yes, blast it, that heavy hulk would be left behind, dash it, no matter how it huffed and puffed – and off they'd go right past!'

'Filly hey! Don't you know who's driving you? Huh? huh? Who's driving? Huh?' and Matti rose to his knees in the sleigh and hit the mare on the rump with the back of the reins, hit her and yelled with each stroke: 'Hee ya!'

Something like this had never happened to the mare before, ever, and so she set off at a gallop, as well as she could, but Matti did not let up.

'Hee ya! Hee ya!' Ya! Let the crown come race with his railroad, let the crown come with his railroad... 'Ya! Ya! Ya!' And Matti lifted the reins high up in the air, shouting and thinking *if only there were a bell on the crossbar – if only there were a bell on the crossbar!*

And the mare galloped with her ears laid back, up and down the hills without stopping... and the snow pelted Matti's eyes more heavily... and got in his mouth, but Matti just thought, *let it come!*

When they came to the base of Marjomäki Hill as they arrived at the village of Valkeiskylä, the mare continued to gallop, although Matti had sat down by then.

'Good Lord, don't run me down!' yelled a woman's voice from in front of the horse, and at the same moment the sleigh zipped past someone who had jumped to the side of the road.

'Who's that not getting out of the road?'

'Good sir, take me into your sleigh!'

'I'm headed up the hill!'

'Aye, I'll walk up the hill all right but ride down the other side.'

Matti stopped his horse. It had grown dim.

'Hey, is that Matliena there? I didn't recognize you in the dark. Climb on in; there's room.' Matti had recognized the woman walking on the road as Liena the masseuse.

'I can... I can get along... back here on the runners... for such a short trip,' Liena panted on Matti's neck. 'Put the bundle in the sleigh. An old woman like me having to walk in the winter cold... they didn't even give me a horse. The master drove off, off after drink – but how could he have if I hadn't worked on his stomach? But it's God's own truth that I won't go doing it again... even if he bursts on the spot! I'm not going to go softening him up again.'

'Where is Miss Matliena coming from?'

'Apparently there isn't a horse in the Huttula stable for a masseuse... I would have had to wait until Sunday to get to my own village with the churchmen. But since my own alderman's wife sent word to come along on Saturday.'

'So they wouldn't give you a horse?'

'No, and I didn't go begging him. Since they didn't realize themselves, I thought that...'

'So the master was off driving?'

'He went right from under my hands. I hadn't even cupped his sides, and he just jumped in the sleigh without even asking...'

'He went off to the railroad?'

'Who cares where he went, the fatbelly.'

'I heard he went to the railroad to fetch some goods. Has Miss Matliena been to see the railroad?'

'Not me... what would an old person like me do running all over the place like that?'

'You really should go, Matliena.'

'I should, I should. Last Sunday three families from our village drove by the church, off to see the railroad. They say you can see it at Lapinlahti church – you don't have to go any farther than that.'

'That is the place to see it.'

'Have you seen it, Matti?'

'Seen it? I may have seen a little of it... '

'Were you off just to see a new thing, or did you have other business?'

'Other business.'

'Is it true what they say about it running with wheels on even in the winter?'

'Is that so! Yes, yes I imagine they do... yes... I haven't been in the winter. What would take me there in the winter?'

'I had thought the same thing, that if the Creator graces us with another summer I could go see it and Lapinlahti church at one go. I have a nephew in Lapinlahti, too.'

The road ran through Valkeiskylä. Before the alderman's porch, Matliena climbed off the runners, took the bundle from the sleigh, and told Matti to send her regards to Liisa.

Matti drove the sleigh forward, scraping along a little farther on the main road, then turning to go through the Mähöläs' yard and then across the field behind the Pitkäläs' sauna. They were already bathing there. The slap of the bath whisks* was audible, and steam billowed out into the cold. Behind the sauna there was a steep bank down to the ice of Naulalampi Pond. The mare's hind legs, being unshod, started to slip a little on the slick slope, but they could make it if they descended steadily – and steadily the mare descended.

It had slowly grown completely dark. The stars twinkled in the sky, and on this night they twinkled extraordinarily brightly. Every now and then one would break away and slide down the canopy of the sky. From the pond the road rose to a meadow, and from there it dropped into a pitch-black forest. Twisting and turning it then ran through more open places, sometimes past clearings, sometimes along a ridge, sometimes through meadows from barn to barn. The cold increased, trying to cover the horse's flanks and the man's eyebrows with frost. Sometimes there would be a rustling fir tree, sometimes a snapping from the corner of a barn. Matti was hunched over in the back of the sleigh with the collar of his fur coat turned up. The mare got free rein to walk the familiar road, but Matti himself was still inspecting the starry canopy of the sky. His eye wandered from the Evening Star, moving to the familiar Otava**, resting on the North Star, and inspecting the Sieve*** and Väinämöinen's Scythe*. But every time a star came loose, sliding downward, Matti said, 'Ha!' and then he would twitch the ends of the reins to send the horse into a canter... but he cursed no more than that while the mare still walked... because Matti was no longer inclined to worry about his horse...

Matti thought there were so many strange things in this world that he could not quite understand – does anyone really understand, though they think themselves wise, these pastors and these pastors' wives? At least he had never before heard such things as these – nowadays it seemed as if there was never any talk but of strange things,  each one more so than the last. Just so long as they did not grow too wise and end the world. So said the old pastor, that before the end of the world people would become too wise, the devil leading them on and showing them all the pageantry of the world from the pinnacle of the temple. But then – 'Ha!' – then lightning cometh out of the east – 'Ha!' – and shineth even unto the – 'Ha!' – west. The stars were so thick now in the heavens. They had never been like that before! Matti greatly feared the end of the world, and little else – but the end of the world would come like a thief in the night... But it would not come yet, since he was on his guard and thinking of it; it would come when no one paid it any mind. People should always think of it, keeping the Lord in their minds and praying to him, crying for his aid.

The mare set off trotting down the ridge, from which the road descended into a low-lying woodland. It was such a dark, thick copse of spruce that the sky could not be seen. Here and there a single star twinkled through the boughs. That winter was a big snow winter, and it was almost like the trees and bushes were drowsing, the tops of the trees' boughs under a

mass of snow. It was almost as if Matti were driving under a canopy. And little by little the noiseless silence of the wood and the monotonous crackling of the runners began to cause Matti to yawn. His eyelids began to feel heavy. The horse and the journey vanished from his mind, along with the rest of the world – all of the miracles and the stars falling from the sky.

His head sank against the side of the sleigh, and Matti slept.

And dreamed.

He saw himself as a small boy, as he had been before when he was an errand boy at the parsonage during the time of the old pastor. The big parsonage gate was open, and Matti was standing guard. The foreman had ordered him to stand there and placed two flags in his hand, a red one and a white one, and said, 'When you see the pastor's carriage driving behind the sacristy, then show the red flag. If the pigs are in the herb garden, but if you can get them driven out, then show the white so the pastor can drive straight into the yard.' So the foreman had said, repeating many times, and then going to hide himself around the corner, where he lurked, watching. Matti stood and looked at the flags, letting the wind wave them. But then suddenly he heard the church bells ringing, even though it was the middle of the week and not a holy day, and when he looked towards the back of the sacristy there was the pastor's carriage coming at a full gallop. But then at the porch they stopped, and the driver waved his hand and yelled, 'Shall we come or not?' But then Matti could not remember if he had driven the pigs from the herb garden, and he was overcome by anxiety and fear of the foreman, and he started to wave both flags, first the red and then the white and then both. The horses broke away from the porch, galloping towards him, the driver unable to rein them in. But when they were a little way away from the gate, one side of the gate closed and the carriage slammed into it, and the driver flew on his face onto the ground. Then the foreman charged around the corner, boxing Matti on the ear, and the driver jumped up from the ground and boxed Matti on the other ear.

Matti's mare had been given free rein to run, and the closer it felt it was getting to home the faster it went. When the forest road ended and a meadow opened up before them, the mare set into a trot, as best it could. But at the gate to the field it extended its tail, let out a quick neigh and stretched out into a full gallop towards the farmyard. But what does a mare understand about avoiding corners? The side of the sleigh slammed against the corner of the cottage so hard that splinters flew from both. Matti's head banged limply first against one side of the sleigh and then the other, and when he awoke he felt as if he had been clouted about both ears.

The mare ran straight to the front of the cottage. Liisa was standing at the door, a wooden torch* in her hand, watching her husband's arrival in amazement.

'Whoa, wo-whoa!' Matti searched the darkness with his eyes. He saw someone standing at some door waving something red over her head.

'I didn't mean... I meant... I just...'

'What are you blathering about?'

'Who's that there waving red? Don't wave red, old woman; they can't come!'

'Huh? They can't come! Who can't come?'

'The pastor's carriage can't.'

'The pastor's carriage? You're still asleep. Do you hear? You're asleep and the mare drove your sleigh into the corner of the cottage!'

'It wasn't my fault.'

'What wasn't your fault?'

'Nothing – the gate did it by itself.'

Liisa went and jerked Matti by the arm, holding the torch in front of his eyes.

'Hey, old man! What are you on about? Are you still sleeping or are you drunk?'

'I'm not sleeping. What are you on about?'

'Well, you must have been sleeping a moment ago when you drove your sleigh into the corner of the cottage.'

'Don't lie! You don't have to be asleep for that to happen...'

'And where is your hat?'

'On my head...' and Matti grabbed at his hat, but it was not on his head.

'There it is, there in the sleigh. Put it on your head so you don't freeze. If it had fallen on the road... What kind of a man falls so soundly asleep in his sleigh that he's dead to the world!'

'You keep your mouth shut about me being asleep. I know best.'

Now Liisa just had to laugh at that – as if he had not been asleep. Even then he was hardly yet awake.

'I could hear your snores all the way across the field, you were sleeping so soundly,' Liisa said mockingly.

'Who was snoring? Not me.'

'Good Lord. Who could it have been, if not you!'

'Maybe you were snoring...'

'Oh, it was me now? Now, when I was just coming from milking in the cowshed?'

But Matti had gotten his horse unharnessed and went to take it to the stable.

Liisa was left to unload the sleigh, holding the burning torch in her teeth.

There was still a good amount of grain in the bottom of the sack. Had she not said to him as he left that he did not need to take a full two bushels? But he just had to have two bushels – he said he would not presume to carry less on his back to the storehouse. Of course. He wanted to show off his strength. And they had not provided any feed at the parsonage, because the chaff Matti had taken was gone. The new foreman was like that, it seemed. One of the bent stays had broken on the side of the sleigh when it drove into the corner. And what about the horse blanket? That pig again! – What?! And now Liisa saw something that truly did not please her, and she yelled to Matti in the stable.

'Good God! Matti! My spinning is still here in the bottom of the sleigh – the work that was supposed to go to the pastor's wife! Do you hear, you knothead, why didn't you give it to the pastor's wife?'

Matti had started preparing feed for his mare and now came to fetch the meal bag from the sleigh.

'Why didn't you give my spinning to the pastor's wife?'

'I did... .'

'Oh, you did? There it is untouched under the hay. You haven't even moved it. There it is, heh!' and Liisa angrily threw the bundle back into the sleigh.

'I didn't remember.'

'You didn't remember! I said that you wouldn't remember. You should have taken me along; then I would have remembered. And now there it is, and what will the pastor's wife say?'

'Was there that much of a rush?'

'Of course there was a rush. That was why I sent it with you.'

'What was it about this time? I've remembered before. I even talked to the pastor's wife, but somehow when I was leaving it slipped my mind.'

'Slipped your mind! What are you doing with that meal bag?'

'For the mare's feed.'

'You're still sleepwalking, you are – there's already feed in the manger. I got it ready.'

Matti went back into the stable. Liisa took the bundle of spinning, the sheepskins, and the sacks out of the sleigh and took them into the cottage.

A little while later Matti came from the stable and inspected the sleigh, seeing that one of the bent stays on the side of the sleigh had broken. He detached the sleigh from the pull shafts and took it to the wall of the stable and upturned it. But then, just by chance, as he was arranging it there, he thought, *it isn't going to go rolling away*. But then he realized that was an utterly senseless idea, not understanding how an idea like that had gotten into his head. He was already about to go to the cottage when he scratched behind his ear and then went to the corner that he had driven his sleigh into. A good chunk of wood had splintered loose. Matti tore it the rest of the way off and then shoved it into a crack in the wall. Then he went into the cottage.

Liisa was straining milk into pails at the corner of the table. The cat circled her, meowing periodically. Matti took off his heavy clothes and then sat down on the bench with his head in his hands. Liisa glanced at him now and then over her strainer and thought, *what is he up to now*, but did not ask. Had he been drinking and was hung over? But she had not smelled any of it on his breath just now. He could not have been drinking. When would he have had the time, since he left this very morning? The cat stole over to Matti and rubbed its side against Matti's boots, meowing quietly. But Matti did not seem to see the cat. *There must be something wrong with him, since he isn't even petting the cat*, thought Liisa.

'Head for the sauna,' Liisa said to Matti as she was pouring the milk into the pail through the sieve for the last time.

Matti ran his fingers through his hair and began to undress for the sauna. He did not say anything, and neither did Liisa. He hurried through the door into the yard, and a little while later Liisa followed.

However, she first poured some milk into the cat's bowl and set it on the floor in front of the hearth; she also lit a new torch and set it in the holder on the corner of the hearth.

And then no one was left in the cottage but the cat lapping at its milk and the torch burning in its clamp. The cat lapped up its warm milk, daintily and soundlessly. The torch crackled as it burned leisurely, and as it did more coils of soot collected the longer it burned. But when it came to a knot where a branch had been, a small tongue of flame leaped from it, sputtering upward and downward. And then the end of the cat's tail would move secretively. But when it had lapped up its milk, cleaned its bowl, and licked its lips, it set off moving about the cottage. It walked with inaudible steps from the hearth to the table. From there it slunk to the women's side of the room*, and then, circling back to the hearth, squinted its green eyes against the light of the torch and meowed a little. Then it went to the end of the table again, hopped on to the bench, and sniffed the milk jug. But then it jumped down to the floor again. Next to the hearth it meowed wretchedly, as if lamenting its plight, and hopped back up on the hearth. There it stretched its neck – longer and longer, crouching lower and lower, and then jumped on to the top of the stove. The torch began sputtering again in its holder; the soot crackled, and a soft purring began to come from on top of the stove.

Matti and Liisa did not say much of anything in the sauna. Matti was already on the sauna bench when Liisa came in. Liisa dipped a bath whisk in water and handed it to Matti.

'Hey, here's a whisk!' she said.

'More?' she asked a little while later and threw more water on the rocks.

'Again,' Matti said.

Liisa continued throwing water onto the hot rocks of the stove...

'Still?'

When Matti did not answer, Liisa threw some more.

'No. Ah! No more... whoaho! No more!' Matti finally said and poured water over his head.

'It was only a little,' said Liisa, but she thought to herself that his skin really could take a lot.

Liisa and Matti still did not speak as they ate their evening meal. Matti ate his curds, but often absentmindedly left his spoon in his cup, not remembering to put another piece in his mouth after he had swallowed the last. Liisa asked him now and then, 'Why aren't you eating,' to which Matti quickly answered, 'I am eating,' and ate. Liisa would have liked to tease Matti about the sleeping, but then she thought, *I'll tease him tomorrow*, and did not tease him.

After eating, Matti's mood was somewhat lighter. It had been very heavy before eating, even in the sauna. He was already thinking about mentioning something about the railroad to Liisa. However, he did not say anything – perhaps she would not believe it and would say he had been dreaming, or something else entirely. She could always find the words.

As she was clearing the food from the table, Liisa said she had taken a hare.

She couldn't stand not to visit my traps, thought Matti, but did not say anything other than to ask a moment later in which trap it had been.

It had been at the corner of the fence, the corner by the burn-beaten meadow, not the corner by the forest – and not in trap but a snare.

But Matti did not remember there being any snare there. In the autumn before it froze, there had been, but he remembered taking them in around the time of the harvest festival.*

'Well, you hadn't brought it in, because the hare found it,' Liisa said and bragged on about how lucky she had been that it fell into the snare. And there had only been one set of tracks, straight from the patch of forest across the meadow, and without any previous path.

Matti did not feel like saying anything any more when he heard that a hare had walked straight into a summer snare. A thing like that meant nothing good – things like that happened before great wars and times of persecution, stars falling from the sky and hares running into summer traps. In the proper order of things, they did not happen at all. And she should not have taken it out of the snare – it should have been left alone. Whatever drove it there would have come to collect it.

It was probably the same one who set steam to walking the earth and then rode it – the other man, not the right one, the one who created the earth.

'What's bothering you, Matti? You aren't sleeping.' Liisa grunted drowsily, pulling the blanket over to her side.

'I am sleeping,' Matti said.

'No, you aren't – you've been groaning all night, tossing back and forth.'

'Something is just keeping me up. Maybe I'm not well.'

'There's no... nothing wrong with you. It's no wonder you aren't sleepy when you were sleeping the whole way back in the sleigh.'

'I didn't sleep the whole way.'

'Even half way… but be quiet now and go to sleep.'

Liisa was very sleepy. She drew the blanket up to her ears again and slept.

Matti mumbled, 'If you knew, you wouldn't feel like sleeping either.'

But then soon he fell asleep himself.

III.

*A*fter rising from his bed the next morning, Matti was in quite a peaceful state of mind and decided to tell Liisa about what he had heard at the parsonage. But Liisa did not stop in one place the whole morning through, moving about her chores in the outdoor kitchen and cowshed. Matti was mending his shoes and thinking *I'll tell her while we're eating breakfast – then she'll have time to listen.* But when Matti was about to start, Liisa was off again, and Matti did not want to say anything about it until Liisa had settled down in one place to listen.

Matti went to his woodpile behind the stable, always peering around the corner to see if Liisa had let off walking between the outdoor kitchen and the cottage. She just kept on walking. And she had not even lighted the fire in the cottage yet ... surely she meant to heat it this morning? The wind was cold enough that they could certainly stand to warm the cottage – so they could go in and warm their hands.

And then Liisa came to fetch wood from the pile ... finally. She would probably sit down at her spinning wheel now.

When the wind started to make smoke stream from the smoke vent into the yard, Matti went in to warm up. He whacked his billhook into a pine log and thought *if she doesn't believe me, then let her not believe me ... it isn't like it's an article of faith.*

The stove was heating, flames blazing from its mouth, now and then setting the soot to smouldering. Matti threw his leather mitts onto the hearth, took a pipe from his breast pocket, split a piece of kindling, and used it to get fire from the stove. Then he warmed his hands over the flames, watching the smoke rippling at the level of the windows.*

Liisa had set up under the window on her side of the room to spin. Matti lifted the tobacco cutter from under the bench and began to chop the leaves.

'Have you already smoked everything that you chopped the day before last?' Liisa asked.

Of course he had not smoked it all – he was just chopping to warm himself.

And Matti chopped tobacco and drew smoke from his pipe, both with equal vigour. He really was drawing at it with singular intensity. He was sucking so hard that the whole contents of the bowl burned as one crackling mass.

Maybe she won't believe me ... but if she doesn't believe me, let her not believe me! It's all the same whether she believes or not ...

'Now they have a railroad at the Lapinlahti church too ... have you heard?'

But Liisa was spinning so intently, and the spinning wheel was droning so loudly, that she did not quite hear what Matti said.

'They have a what?'

Matti tried to speak in as disinterestedly a manner as possible.

'Oh, just a railroad – the folks over in Lapinlahti parish have gotten a railroad. Apparently they built it for them there since they had asked the crown, so they wouldn't have to go anywhere by horse, either in summer or in winter. I don't know if it's true, what they were saying...'

'Goodness gracious, don't go tearing pieces out of the new broom I just put on that handle ... there are older ones around too! Why were you pulling at it?'

'My pipe is clogged...'

As he spoke, Matti had drawn on his pipe so hard it had clogged, and while he talked he had gone over to the corner to fetch a twig.

'Well wouldn't a twig from the old broom have done just as

well? In any case, what were you saying the folks in Lapinlahti had made?'

'They didn't make anything, but the crown has built them a railroad, which they can take as far as Helsinki or even America.'

'To where?'

'To America.'

'Don't go telling lies now, husband.'

Liisa stopped her spinning wheel and looked over the wheel at Matti, eying him like the sort of liar whose words do not have even the slightest basis in fact.

But at this Matti lost his temper, and he broke the twig inside the pipe stem.

'What are you looking at? If you don't believe me, then so be it, but as for me I'm going to go see it soon. It's a peculiar sight to see, and if you don't want to come along, then don't come. I'm not going to go nagging at you...'

'So you're going to go see the folks from Lapinlahti set off for America? I hear that's exactly where people have been leaving from for America!' And from behind Liisa's spinning wheel came a mocking snort.

'No, I'm going to see the railroad – that's a sight to see in itself.'

'Is it as amazing a thing to see as the panorama in the parlour at the parsonage you nagged me to go see?'

'I haven't nagged you to go anywhere. You wanted to go see that yourself.'

'No, I didn't...'

Matti laughed with a sneer. 'Is that so ... well, we'll see who wants to do what this time.' It was impossible not to laugh at Liisa's stupidity ...

'It isn't any old panorama. Who said anything about a panorama?'

'Well, what is it?'

'It's a railroad.'

'Well, what's a railroad then? ... Nothing.'

'Nothing, is it! Women don't understand anything. They're so stupid and simpleminded that you can't do anything with them ... even a ram has more sense than a woman. Oh, so a railroad isn't anything? How do you know better than me, who heard it with my own ears?'

But Liisa had taken offense now and was kicking her spinning wheel violently. And Matti chopped, so hard that a dusting of flakes floated to the floor.

'Liisa!' Matti said a little while later, but Liisa did not answer.

'Liisa!' Matti said again.

'Well then, say what you have to say!'

'It probably won't help even if I do say it to you.'

'Then don't!'

But Matti couldn't stand not to. A little while later he said it, stopping his chopping, explaining just as if holding her by the hand.

'Now stop, Liisa – listen while I explain. A railroad is a rail road and a dirt road is a dirt road ... a normal road is made of dirt and mud and a rail road is made of iron rails...'

'And a wood road from wood and a water road from water?' And again she gave a mocking snort.

But Matti did not get angry.

'Don't start now. It's all true; it's just like I said. I bet you don't know how they drive on the railroad ... by horse, perhaps?'

But Liisa did not have any idea. She spun and listened, sometimes looking at Matti scornfully, but thinking, *let him talk, and we'll see what sorts of lies he's fallen for this time.*

'No, not by horse, no, never! Another kind of road will have to do for the horses. Now that they've made a road of iron!'

'An iron road? Ha!'

Matti started to get angry again.

'Out of iron, out of iron – if you don't believe me, then go ahead and don't believe me...They made it out of sheets and rails of iron. Hm! That's right, out of iron ... and when you make a road of that, then you've got to have the vehicles and the things that do the pulling along it. A steam boat, a machine like the *Suomela* is dragged on land and put on wheels, and it moves powered by fire and pulls carriages after it – as big as this cottage and bigger – it can pull any kind. And the road doesn't shake – that's what it's like!'

'Poor Matti, who has been playing you for a fool this time?'

'No one has. No one ever has!'

'Then you're making up these lies in your own head. At least you could have lied more sensibly ... you can't even lie properly, poor man.'

Matti was startled ... *you'll give up thinking you know what's what when you hear who told me,* he thought.

'Is it a lie or the truth? If it is a lie, then better people than me have lied before, and I'm just repeating what they said – I don't know anything of myself. The pastor's wife's words they are,' said Matti, sighing humbly and then settling back to cutting up tobacco.

'The pastor's wife? Had the pastor's wife really said that?'

Now Liisa's spinning wheel stopped, and now she really opened her ears.

'The pastor and his wife,' Matti added.

'Really ... ?'

'The pastor and his wife told me. I didn't hear about it from anyone else.'

'No ... really?'

'They were the ones who told me. They had just been to see it, gone just for that purpose.'

'Well, what did they say?'

Now it was Matti's chance to be grand... .

'What did they say? They said what I already told you, even though you didn't believe me.'

'That there's a road made out of sheets of iron there?'

'Exactly, and that a machine lifted up on wheels moves along it.'

'The *Suomela*?'

'That it may be. Instead of blades it has wheels, big wheels and small wheels, all of which are moved by the power of fire.'

'But I don't believe that, that fire makes it move!'

'Well, that's what it does – just like when it moves through the water...'

'Let them do what they may, but that I won't believe, not even when it moves through the water.'

'Don't you believe the pastor? Do you think you are more wise than the pastor?'

'I'm not ... but even the pastor's wife said she didn't believe last summer when there was talk about it moving without any oars.'

'Now she does, now that she's seen it moving on land as well.'

'She believes it now? And that they lifted it up on wheels? Now there is a bit of building!'

'The crown's men can build anything!'

'The crown's men built it?'

'They did indeed!'

'Well, what were they doing taking it to the Lapinlahti

church? They could have brought it here to our own church, then when we went to church we could have seen it. They haven't brought it here yet, have they? If we knew when they would bring it here, we could go see... .'

'I don't know if they'll bring it ... there wasn't any talk of it.'

'So even the pastor's wife has been to see it?'

'They left in the morning and were there by midday. They said that I should go see it too.'

'Do you mean to go?'

'I don't know. An old man like me?'

'Didn't they say anything about me?'

'There wasn't any talk of you.'

'It sure would be a strange contraption, if it really is like that. Will we see it before we die? But what if you're lying?'

'I'm not lying. Have I ever lied before? Can you tell me when?'

'No, no ... but don't you think it would be a strange contraption?'

'What's so strange about it? We've seen and heard stranger things.'

'But surely nothing like this?'

But now Matti thought he had chopped enough tobacco and went out again to his logs. As he pulled his billhook from the log, he said to himself scornfully, 'So she did believe me – and why not, since it was true. Even an emperor would have to believe.'

Liisa was left alone in the cottage. She spun for a while, kicking the spinning wheel so violently and tugging the fibre from the distaff so angrily that every now and then it broke in her hand. And then it was always a bother to join it. How had such weak spots gotten onto the distaff? It was always breaking. And the yarn wouldn't stay on the wheel either! What poorly dressed flax the parsonage was supplying, with so much lint ... what sort of flax was this, anyway? The spinning wheel started whirring again, even faster, the treadle creaking and the white mark on the wheel becoming a single line, a whole pile of thread collecting on the spool in no time at all. Liisa wound it out, the spool eating it ever more greedily.

Almost half of the distaff had been spun ... but then the spool suddenly devoured all of the thread at once, sending the distaff flying. The yarn slipped from the wheel, and Liisa had to leave off kicking, but then the treadle starting sprinting with such a horrible noise that it seemed like it might break on the spot . The whole spinning wheel was useless, -- let it stand idle in the corner! Liisa fairly tossed her spinning there and then went to pull a coal from the stove. And how the little devils were burning. Ouch! Hot enough to burn the eyes out of your head...

Liisa closed the smoke vent and looked out the window into the yard. The sleigh was out there turned over against the stable wall, its metal skids shining in the sun ... and the tip of Matti's billhook flashed now and then from around the corner.

Liisa sighed a very long sigh ... what was she sighing about anyway? She didn't really know herself. Reluctantly she went back to her spinning wheel and began untangling the messy spool. It was very tangled – and then the end of her nose started itching just as she was almost done untangling the mess... .

But what of that batch of spinning and all the rest? Though she spun as much as she could, the spinning still did not get where it should, no matter how many times she sent it. Who ever heard such a thing? The man goes to deliver the spinning, but does not have the sense to actually deliver it? Strange, since he remembered to pay his grain. He should have forgotten that too, all in one go!

Liisa went and snatched the bundle of spinning Matti had forgotten to give to the pastor's wife from the stove shelf. She set it next to the bench and untied it. There they were, the skeins and balls arranged so nicely ... the skeins and balls ... it was such a shame the pastor's wife had not even seen them. *At least he could have taken me along. But what did he go and do, going himself but still not getting things delivered? What will the pastor's wife think? She had asked for it so insistently. She might be thinking all sorts of horrible things, if she wished.* And Liisa started feeling almost as if she should go deliver them right then – by foot if necessary. Matti might give her the horse of course; that would not be too much, giving her the horse. He might for the pastor's wife's sake, since she might be waiting for her yarn.

So the good pastor's wife had been to see the railroad. There was surely no better person in the entire world than the pastor's wife. It must be some contraption indeed, the railroad. Had the pastor's wife found it a strange sight? And at Christmas she had said that when Matti came to make the lease payment she should send the spinning with him. And then she would get new work in its place. What was she thinking now that it was not sent after all? She might be thinking all sorts of things, if she wished!

As they were eating their midday meal, Liisa looked very concerned. Then she suddenly said, 'That's it, there's nothing for it but to leave this very night to take the spinning to the pastor's wife.'

'Huh?' Matti said, continuing to eat.

'I said that no matter what you say, there's nothing for it ... nothing at all,' Liisa said determinedly, folding her knife and putting it in her pocket.

'What's the rush with it now?' Matti said, still eating. 'Won't there be time later?'

It was good that he was not objecting any more than that. Liisa had been afraid that he would not even hear of it.

'We should already have taken it, a long time ago, and it's just got left behind. You're quite the businessman! And what will I do in the meantime? Turn an empty spinning wheel?'

'You could start spinning the net cords.'

'Which we already have more of than you'll ever get woven!'

'So what have you been spinning yesterday and today? Spin that!'

'And this old beast of a spinning wheel – nothing comes of spinning linen with it, especially when the flax is so poorly dressed.'

'Would wool be better?'

'And since the pastor's wife was intending to weave cloth ...

wasn't it this week! Where will she get the weft, when it's here?'

Matti did not reply. He was still just eating and drinking buttermilk from his mug. Liisa was starting to get fed up with the incessant eating and drinking.

'We should take it this very day!'

'Well, I'm not about to go a second time.'

'You don't need to. I could go, if you give me the horse... .'

'You?' (and then from inside his mug), 'Who will take care of

the cow?'

'As if you hadn't taken care of it often enough before...'

'That mare might go wild and gallop, and you couldn't stop it.'

'I know how to drive the mare just as well as you do. And I

wouldn't drive it...'

' ... into any corners,' Liisa was about to say, but then thought, *what if he gets angry?* and didn't.

'How wouldn't you drive it?'

'Oh, nothing ... hmmm, what was I saying? Oh, that one of us really should go tonight!'

'Tonight? In the dead of night?'

Good, Liisa thought.

'If not tonight, then at the latest early in the morning.'

Matti did not say anything. He stopped eating and started preparing his pipe. He did not seem to be agreeing, but he was also not forbidding it. After a little while, he said, 'Ask the pastor, if you happen to see him ... I mean ask through his wife, if she doesn't know herself, what kinds of wheels the carriages have, big and small. I didn't happen to ask. Tell the pastor's wife to ask the pastor.'

'Oh, I'm sure I'll be able to ask the pastor himself. I've spoken to him many times before. Should I also ask if they're going to bring the railroad to our church too?'

'No, I already know they won't. No need even to ask – it can't be brought over just like that.'

'We don't know for sure. We'll know for sure if we ask. I think it's good to ask.'

You can go ahead and ask, Matti thought, *but they won't be bringing it every place ... And yet if ...* he thought then, but he did not say anything to Liisa.

And so all that day Liisa was in such a good mood that it almost made her stomach ache. It was almost enough to make her jump up and down, old though she was. Every now and then a laugh almost burst out of its own accord, even though she did not know just why each time – usually because of her own thoughts. And everything just felt so good. Even the spinning wheel spun just like always, and the yarn did not slip off the wheel even once.

And Liisa felt so good about Matti that she boiled coffee, heated the sauna – even though she had the day before – put butter on the table when they were eating supper, and made conversation about the railroad, letting Matti do the telling. Matti and Liisa continued to sit long after supper, one sitting at the end of the table smoking his pipe and the other brushing her hair on the edge of the bed. They watched the cat lap its milk on the corner of the hearth, lick its bowl, clean its tongue, and go slinking around the cottage. Then they took turns stroking it, and Matti picked it up and scratched it under the chin, making it purr. And they chatted about the railroad, chatting about this brand new miracle, this strange thing ... about there being no end to the things one hears in one's old age. *We may see it yet*, Liisa thought, but Matti said they could believe it without seeing just as well, to which Liisa did not reply. But then when the cat had purred for a while on the stove, they extinguished the torch and lay down on the bed.

But Liisa was so strangely alert that night. Matti was already asleep, and the cat's spinning wheel was still droning its even drone on the stove, but Liisa could not seem to get any sleep. She heard even the smallest rustling in the cottage walls; she heard if a cockroach accidentally fell from the ceiling to the floor; and she heard the muffled stamping of the mare's foot when she stirred in her stall. She could pick out the lighter hole of the window from the rest of the wall and a star twinkling through it; and when she pulled the covers up to her ears or closed her eyes, she still thought she could hear and see everything. She lay there full awake, thinking about whether it might already be time to get up and prepare provisions for the next day, but she was afraid Matti might wake up and ask what she was doing, so she did not get up. Finally she slept, but in the morning before the crowing of the cock she awoke and began preparing for her departure.

IV.

*M*atti had sent Liisa on her trek in the grey light of dawn. He had gone and rocked the sleigh into place, filled it with hay, put fodder in the bag, led the mare from the stable, and harnessed her. Then he had set Liisa in the sleigh, covered her with blankets, handed her the reins, and ordered the mare to set off. The mare had pushed a little against its collar, and the sleigh had started to move. Matti had remained standing where the sleigh had been, his hands hanging at his sides, watching the mare's progress until it was halfway across the field. But then Liisa had suddenly exclaimed from within her shawls, 'Good God!' and stopped the mare. Matti had asked, 'What's wrong?' To this Liisa had shouted back, 'I left the bundle ... the bundle of spinning ... it's under the back window on the bench. Whoa!' Matti had gone and taken the bundle from the bench under the back window and carried it to Liisa, and then Liisa had set off driving and disappeared into the morning gloom.

But Matti had gone back into the cottage again, lain down, and slept long into midday.

Then he had risen, stretched, yawned, looked out one window into the yard, then from another – and gone back to bed.

However, he did get up to eat. And eat he did, although in a leisurely fashion; what would he be in a rush for? He especially ate a lot of butter and swigged buttermilk from his mug, mixed with half a measure – more than half – of milk.

Then, after eating, he went to the cowshed. He did have to

look in on the cow – was there food? There she was mooing at Matti in her crib, and the manger was empty. Matti threw some hay in, but did not bother watering the cow; let Liisa give her water when she comes...

But it did not appear that Liisa would come back that day, and Matti had to water and milk the cow himself.

After milking the cow, eating his dinner, and drinking some warm milk, Matti went to cut some torches before going to bed. But his torch cutting knife was very dull, very dull indeed, and he did not have anyone to turn the grinding wheel to sharpen it. The block of wood was frozen too ... let it wait to thaw tomorrow ... and there were torches still up there on the beam! Matti carried the torch billet back to the corner, drove his knife into a hole in the window frame, and then hammered it in even more securely with the base of his palm.

Matti felt completely rested when he awoke. The previous night he had been very tired, so very tired, but now he was not tired at all any more. As he waited for daybreak, Matti began to cut torches again. And now they split nice and thin – had the wood melted, or had the knife grown sharper in the wall!

As the day began to break, Matti began to listen for Liisa's homecoming. He went out to the yard and stood near the corner of the cottage. She should already have been here if she had left after rising early, as they had discussed.

But there was no sign of Liisa, and Matti had to milk the cow and make it ready for the day.

Matti thought about what he should do, but there was not any sort of work that he really had a mind to do all day. Even chopping wood was not something that had to be done every day. Matti thought he might go into the forest to check his hare traps, and this is what he decided to do. What if something had happened to set one off with a foot? That had even happened to Liisa when Matti was not home! Who knows, perhaps now as well?

After eating his breakfast – he had fried himself some potatoes over the stove – Matti prepared to go into the forest to his traps. He took his skis down from the wall of the cottage and began to fit his foot into the straps. The skis were fitted for Liisa; she had used them last. Look at that – had she put a notch in one of the bindings? Hadn't been able get the ice to come off the place where her foot went otherwise and had to use a hatchet? A chip had come off the binding of one of the skis, a big chip. It looked just as if she had first skied so long that banging it with the pole was no longer enough to dislodge the ice and then had carried the skis into the cottage to melt and straighten; she had done that once before!

Matti skied behind the sauna and across the field towards the forest along the existing tracks. Matti had the first trap at the corner of the field closest to the house; not much ever got into it, but that was not why it was there. If it had not been there, nothing would have gone into the other snares either – that was why it was there; such was Matti's superstition.

Matti skied on from the field into the forest. There he had traps in three places, three in each. A little way into the forest there was an open place where Matti and Liisa had felled some leafy trees in the summer and made bundles of twigs with leaves for the animals to eat, and bath whisks. On moonlit nights the hares were drawn there to nibble the bark of the aspens, and there Matti had set his traps in ambush. At the edge of the clearing he had put one under a track, in the place where the hare, creeping silently from the forest, squatted to listen, to decide if he dared come out. Three paths led to the clearing, and a trap had been placed at the mouth of each. Something had always hit them – a hare a week, sometimes two. But now nothing had; nothing in the two traps that were close to each other.

And nothing had hit the third either. Well, no wonder, as snow had fallen on the path over there. It had fallen from the trees, and who else but Liisa? It must have been her who knocked it from the trees as she passed. She had brushed against the branches ... and a hare will not stand for snow being on the path. Matti checked the path more carefully. He knew a hare had been there and turned back when it had found the strange snow on the path. What was Liisa thinking? He had already said she should leave the hare hunting to him, but no – she still goes around secretly when others are away and ruins their hunting luck. And would the hare ever come there again? Hardly, once it had learnt not to.

Matti felt angry as he left his empty traps to ski to the others. But he should not be angry; when you are angry, hares won't hit the traps either.

Might anything have hit the traps near the haystack? The haystack was in a low spot in the meadow. Matti coasted downhill along the hay road to the meadow. He approached the haystack. He did not know yet if anything had hit the traps, since they were on the other side of the haystack. Matti's heart beat a little fast as he attempted to approach the haystack as quietly as possible; would a hare be in the trap? Hardly. Matti had no faith it at all. He had not set off thinking he would get anything; he had just set off skiing for his own amusement. And now the tips of the skis were on the other side of the stack, and Matti was stretching his head around the other side ... Nothing. Blast! Well, he had known it. Nothing – no hare and not even any sign of a hare! The path was all covered too; loose snow had drifted over it in the night and covered the track a long way from the haystack and no hare had been there in many days. Feeling bitter, Matti dug the traps out of the snow with his ski pole and hung them on the tip of a stake on the side of the haystack.

On the other side of the meadow, on the far side of the past autumn's rye field, in a dense stand of fir trees, Matti had his last traps. But he did not feel like going over there. When there was nothing next to the haystack, there would not be anywhere else either – it was a sure sign. It was apparent the hares had not been out.

However, Matti did not turn home. What if he were to go look at the place at the corner of the field where Liisa had gotten that hare! And Matti set off following the track Liisa had made. It was a little snowy. Matti skied towards the strip of forest that was in the centre of the meadow ... and then past it. There was an old set of hare tracks leading out of the forest, and the ski track followed it. But what was this! Right there was a perfectly fresh track. It came from the strip of forest and went right in the same direction as the previous track!

Matti skied faster towards the corner of the fence, where the tracks still led. At least seen from a distance there did not seem to be anything. But when he came closer, he saw that something had been rolling around in the snow next to the fence – now to see if it had been a hare. Perhaps it was on the other side of the fence. Matti could not stand to keep skiing – he was taken with a fear that it might get loose – and he jumped from his skis and waded through the snow up to his waist to the corner of the fence.

But Matti was sorely disappointed. A hare had rolled around in the fresh snow there, but it was nowhere to be seen ... not on the other side of the fence either. There was no sign of it any more. But soon Matti noticed what had happened. The hare had broken the fastener with which the snare was tied. And was it any wonder? She had not thought, the fool, to put a new cord to fasten it. Who knew how long an old fastener would last that had been rotting there all winter? There ... there ... there! And Matti ripped the snare fastener off the stake to which it was tied and threw the stake itself far off into the forest.

No longer could Matti forgive Liisa for having left the old fastener on the snare. It was strange the first hare had not broken it. It probably could have if it had wanted to. But what kind of a hare had it been anyway? Now he could see what hare it was, not tearing the rotten cord, even though it could have. Something must have been controlling it, whatever it was ... a forest spirit ... But this had been a real hare, this last one. That was clear from all the signs, since it had broken the cord.

Matti set off skiing towards home. What business did Liisa have going and checking other people's traps? First she knocks snow on the path ... would it be strange then if no hares came? And then to leave an old cord – it was a wonder if a hare did not break it! And off went the hare with a perfectly good snare around its neck, and would it bring it back? Yes, of course, that must be why it took it!

Matti was irritated, very irritated; and did he not have good reason? He would have liked to know what other hunter would have tolerated women at his traps! Ah, so your missus was out checking the hare traps! It would have been better if she had tripped the trap with her own foot -- then she would have woken up, running around in the forest like that.

Matti skied across the field into the yard. It was a little bit uphill, and his foot nearly slipped out of the binding every now and then. Blast! And then she goes off visiting! To deliver her spinning? As if it had been such a rush ... the pastor's wife certainly would have asked for it if it had been. Liisa had just said that was the reason because she had been eager to hear something about the railroad! And what good will it do if she does hear – she will still be just as stupid!

Matti's foot slipped again, almost making him fall on his nose in the snow. Yeah, the railroad! Was the whole story even true? That was just people talking, things like that! Lies, lies, the whole thing. Saying you could get to Helsinki on it in a day. And to foreign lands! That was impossible ... In a single day? Wouldn't they have to stop over for the night, no matter how they drove and even if they were gentlemen! We'll just see what they say to Liisa. To be sure, she'll believe anything, the foolish woman, and repeat it to anyone to boot.

Matti was just skiing behind the sauna into the yard as Liisa turned her horse around the corner of the cottage.

'Whoa! Hello! Hello! ... whoa! Greetings from the pastor and his wife. Come along, husband, come help. I've sunk so deep in this sleigh that I can't ... whoa! The maidservants at the parsonage covered me and tucked ... me ... in here ... so ... whoa! There she goes ... come hold the horse so she doesn't ... that I ... Hey now! ... Whoa!'

But Matti did not come to hold the horse, and the mare took Liisa all the way to the open-walled shed next to the barn and began to pull hay into its mouth with its lips.

Matti set his skis against the wall of the cottage and said to Liisa, 'What are you doing driving into the shed?' and only then went to back the horse out of the shed.

'Look, I didn't mean it to, it just went ...'

'You should get your horse under control. Hey, hey, hey! What are you up to there, mare? She can't have gotten anything into her mouth for a long time, since she's so hungry.'

'She's had food. She was in the stable the whole time ... and the pastor's wife even instructed the inspector ... they always feed her whenever I visit.'

'Are you planning to get up? Or do you mean to sit there the rest of your days?'

'I can't get out. Lend a hand, Matti.'

'Shall I rock the sleigh over on its side?'

'Good God! Of course not, Matti! Well then don't ... I can get out myself!'

Liisa did get out and went into the cottage. Matti

unharnessed the horse and took it into the stable.

A little while later Liisa appeared at the door of the stable.

'Are you making mash for the mare? That's good ... here, let me mix it.'

'I know how to do it too.'

'Well, I'll get water for her then.'

'She's already drunk. She isn't thirsty.'

'Who knows, she might still drink.'

'She won't drink. Can't you believe me when I say she won't drink!'

'Well don't start ... don't start now.'

And, looking like she was in a good mood, Liisa carried water to the stable from the tub in a bucket and put it before the mare.

'See, she's drinking,' Liisa said.

But Matti just kept sulking, silently stirring the mash.

'Well, aren't you going to ask about my visit, Matti? What if I had heard a lot of news?'

'In two days you might have had time to hear all sorts of things. Strange you felt like leaving already, that you didn't stay longer to listen.'

Liisa turned it into a joke.

'I didn't really want to leave, but finally I had to, because I was worried about how you would get along here missing me, poor old man.'

'But goodness gracious how we sat telling stories last night, the pastor's wife and I! And the pastor often walked through the kitchen with his pipe, even joining the conversation now and then, giving long speeches.'

But Matti pretended not to hear. He delivered the mash to the mare and started mucking out the stable.

'And, oh, that strange contraption, the railroad – we talked all about it, and not about much else. If only you knew what it's like!'

Matti knew just as well as Liisa did, but did not bother to brag. He simply remained silent.

'Will you be off again tomorrow, or shall I harness the mare right now ... before she's eaten her mash?'

But Matti's jibes could not get to Liisa now.

'Not yet, but once the summer comes, then we'll go and that's all there is to it!'

'And where will we be off to in such a hurry then?'

'To Lapinlahti to see the railroad!'

'What railroad?'

'Lord God Almighty, the railroad in Lapinlahti!'

'The railroad that isn't there?'

'Not there?'

'Are you still clinging to the belief that something like that could really exist?'

'Clinging to the belief? What about you then? You believed it.'

'I never believed it – I don't believe hearsay before I see with my own eyes ... and anyone who does is crazy.'

'But the pastor's wife has seen it!'

'The pastor's wife has made a fool of you, because she knows you'll believe anything.'

'And the pastor? Has the pastor been making a fool out of me too? Huh? And the pastor? You don't even believe the pastor?'

'You don't have to shout! I can hear you well enough; I'm not deaf!'

'I'm not even shouting. I'm just asking if you're calling the pastor a liar too.'

'Oh, so I've called him a liar then?'

'He is a liar if he has said that there is a railroad and then there isn't. Then he is a liar!'

'Look, don't start shouting again! What are you doing coming out here in the stable and shouting? Go shout in the barn if you feel like shouting. I'll take care of my horse. You take care of your cow!'

Liisa went, but she felt very bad. She would have so liked to tell him what she had talked about with the pastor and his wife ... and especially since she knew that Matti knew little about the railroad compared to her. But that was why he could not bear to listen, since he knew less. He would have talked easily enough if she had been the one listening.

But we'll speak about it yet, once Matti is in a better mood. He's always like that when he is in a bad mood ...

But it was a long time before Matti wished to improve his mood. He sulked for many a day, looking pensive and ill-tempered. Especially on the days he returned from the forest empty-handed.

All winter he failed to trap more than a single hare at the haystack ... and some miscreant had already eaten half of it.

And whenever Liisa started talking about the railroad, he immediately said, 'Lies! Not another word! I don't believe it!'

And Liisa would have so liked to tell him about it. She had heard much of which Matti surely knew nothing ... about the big and small wheels and the rest. And Liisa would have liked Matti to know what she herself knew. Liisa did not wish to be wiser and more knowledgeable than her husband. They had forgotten to tell Matti about this thing and that thing, the pastor's wife had said, and this especially Liisa would have liked to tell Matti. But as soon as she began doing so, Matti said, 'Lies! Not another word! I don't believe it!'

And this hurt Liisa deeply. She set her spinning wheel to spinning and did not speak to Matti for many days. She made the food and set the table, but did not call Matti to eat. And she did not come to the table to eat with him – only after Matti had eaten did Liisa begin her meal, saying nothing ... and not putting butter on her bread.

After a few more attempts, Liisa held her peace about the railroad all winter, and so did Matti.

But both of them thought of the railroad, even though they did not speak of it. They dreamed of it often and heard each other speaking of it in their sleep. But if they happened to wake from their nocturnal speeches, they would quickly turn their backs to each other, each pulling the blanket over and pretending to sleep.

V.

*B*ut then winter began to turn to spring. The sunshine pressed the snow and drifts lower and lower to the ground. On the hillsides water began to flow from beneath the snow, to flow and flow, until the cold of the night chilled its progress and then the warmth of another day moved it downwards once again.

Finally it did not freeze at all any more – the meltwater gurgled night and day down the slopes, rending all the snow and drifts at once from the fields and fence posts down into the valleys and low places, where the flowering quillworts then sprouted by the hundreds along the brooks, and fresh summer grass pushed up green here and there.

Away melted winter from around Korventausta cottage as well. The snow dripped slowly as water from the roof of the cottage, snowless patches grew about the walls on the sunny sides of the buildings, snowless patches came to the yards, and the rye crop began to appear in the fields. And then, little by little, without anyone noticing, all the land was clear; only next to the woodpile under the wood chips did ice still radiate its cold.

But when Matti cleared the wood chips away and took a pick and broke the ice into small pieces, throwing them around the yard, the sun conquered the scattered band. And the birch behind the cottage began to put out its leaves, and the swallow flew from the direction of the village and swooped into the nest in the stable; and thus, summer had arrived outside Korventausta cottage, the sun shining without ceasing... .

And so also had summer come within its walls. Moods had thawed, and at last their stiffness was no more.

Without ceasing had the sun shone in through the windows, from each in turn. The winter days had begun to feel long, especially Sabbath days. These Matti had endeavoured to wear out in sleep and Liisa in gazing upon the Word. But they could not always sleep or look upon the Word, especially not as the sun warmed the floor and heated the whole room more and more.

On Ascension Day, Matti could not sleep the entire day away. In the afternoon, he rose from lying on the bench, stretched, yawned, and said, 'Oh–ho – now that was a sleep,' and a little smile appeared upon his face.

Liisa sat under the window on her side of the room, looking at the Book, brass glasses on her nose. From there she gazed over her glasses, eying Matti, and said, a little gently, a little reproachfully, 'Indeed it was!'

'But what else is there to do?' Matti said, slapping his hands against his knees and standing up with great effort. He reached for his pipe above the window and went to light it at the stove. Then he leaned his back against the hearth, his hands behind him, smoking and looking into the afternoon sunshine. 'Yes indeed ... if it keeps up like that, the ground will be clear by Pentecost.'

'Who knows?' Liisa replied, putting her book away.

'Now we won't be able to get anywhere from out here in the middle of the woods – you'd sink on the forest roads and the main road is like to be completely clear. No one could drive a horse on any of them or go sloshing around by foot either... who knows when they will be passable.'

Liisa thought for a little while and then wondered to herself, *Should I say it?* and then she did ...

'If there were a railroad from our cottage to the village, then the bad roads wouldn't matter...'. The pastor's wife had said the same thing jokingly, that if there were a railroad, the bad roads wouldn't matter.

And Matti did not say it was a lie. At first he said nothing at all, just looking long at one place in the yard, and then saying in reply, 'Every cottage would need one of them.'

Good, Liisa thought, but did not say anything more on the matter at that time. But soon she had put the pan on the fire, and as they ate supper she sat down with Matti at the table and spread butter upon her bread.

And it was precisely upon the Saturday of Pentecost that Matti cleared the last of the unmelted ice from the side of the woodpile. Liisa had heated the sauna, and together they had bathed, eaten, and stroked the cat, and then begun to tell stories as the evening sun still shone red through the cottage windows.

First came talk of the great holy days, then the Word of God and the promulgators of the Word of God, of priests, both good and bad. Good were the priests from their own parish, the pastor in particular, to Matti's mind.

Liisa also thought that they were good, although she had indeed heard that the priest at Lapinlahti had greater gifts.

'Greater, you say?' Matti did not remember hearing such a thing.

But to that said Liisa, 'greater … much greater … and the people in Lapinlahti have many other good things as well.'

'What do they have that is so good?'

'Well, at least they have the railroads and all.'

'Yes,' Matti agreed, again as if it were an old familiar thing, which they had already spoken of before.

They sat silently for a short time.

Then Matti said, 'It would be a fine thing to go and listen to this more gifted priest in Lapinlahti.'

'To go and listen? But it is rather a long way.'

'It isn't so far – a dozen miles from our church.'*

'When would we go?'

'Perhaps for Midsummer.'

'And the cow?'

'You could fetch some idle old woman from Valkeiskylä to tend it while we're gone.'

And Liisa had nothing more against the idea, if only they could find a person to watch the house so the poor cow would not go unmilked. For once they could try going to hear a priest of another parish, before they died – they could always hear their own parish priests – and what if that perhaps could be some aid to a sinful soul …

And so it was that upon Midsummer Eve Matti and Liisa were setting out for Lapinlahti church to hear the words of this priest with greater gifts.

'Get going … I'll be along!' Liisa yelled to Matti as he stood waiting in the yard. Liisa still had somewhat more to say, whatever it was, to the person they had fetched from Valkeiskylä to guard the house.

Matti threw his birch-bark knapsack over his back and set off. He climbed the ladder over the farmyard fence, which had been built from the corner of the granary to the corner of the cottage, and then walked along the bank of earth beside the field, then the ditch, and then the fence ... and along the fence grew a flourishing raspberry patch. After coming to the gate that led out into the meadow, Matti looked back ... Liisa was already on her way. She was just leaning on a post as she climbed over the farmyard fence. She then collected her skirts and came after him.

Matti did not wait at the gate, but Liisa caught him up. Then they both walked along the meadow road in single file, with Matti ahead and Liisa a bit behind.

'In just a couple of weeks we may be able to start swinging the scythe here,' Matti said. 'Look how the meadowsweet is pushing up along the fence.'

'Sure enough,' Liisa said, trying to keep up. In the dell was a brook, still full of water.

Goodness gracious, how will I get over this?' Liisa said, stopping.

'Walk along the logs,' Matti said, continuing on.

'Yes, but what if I fall – don't leave me behind!'

'You won't fall!'

And Liisa did not fall.

They came out of the meadow lowland to the edge of a broad-leaved wood, from the wood over a bog into a deep forest, and after walking through the forest to higher ground where a pine-covered ridge rose gradually. They travelled quickly, assiduously directing all their strength to walking while they were fresh.

But when they arrived at the ridge, they saw beside the road the big Resting Stump, which marked that they had travelled the first quarter of the journey. Liisa sat down to rest, but Matti pulled his tobacco pouch out from under his waistband and filled his pipe.

'Don't throw the match on the dry moss – it will catch fire, and the whole forest will burn.'

'What would it hurt, then, if it did alight, empty woodland like this?'

'What need is there to go setting it on fire though?'

'Well, no, there is no need,' Matti admitted.

And then they were walking again, down the other side of the ridge, a steeper slope where the forest grew denser and opened up in turns as they walked, and in places the ground echoed hollowly. Then again through broad-leaved woods, sometimes even meadows, although they walked around the meadows along the outermost fence lines. As they approached the main road, a small pine forest began, with the smell of dry needles wafting to the noses of the walkers.

Just as they came to the main road, a magpie sprang from the forest over the road and began to jump from tree to tree, cackling incessantly.

Matti meant to snatch up a broken branch from the roadside and throw it, driving off the magpie. But he did not after all. It occurred to him that perhaps Liisa would believe he thought the magpie was laughing at them, and that he had driven it away because he was annoyed. So Matti pretended not to see the magpie. He just let it go on hopping ahead and laughing. And the magpie cackled and hopped from tree to tree on either side of the road, tittering and dipping its tail. Only when they arrived at the main road did it break company with Matti and Liisa and fly back into the forest.

'It must have had a nest, raising such a racket,' Liisa said.

'That lot are always on about something,' Matti said.

After arriving at the main road, at the crossroads, where there was a snowplough up on its summer blocks at the base of the mile marker, there was another resting place. Liisa sat down on the ditch bank, but Matti sat down on the end of the blade of the snowplough.

'That's a snowplough there,' Liisa said. 'The railroad has a snowplough too.'

'Of course that road has its snowplough like all the other highways.'

'Well, of course. But the railroad's snowplough isn't drawn

by horses.'

'Well, how then?'

'The pastor's wife said the machine pulls that as well.'

'Of course it could; when it goes on the water it has the strength of seven horses.'

'But apparently sometimes it gets stuck in the snow too, so badly it can't budge, no matter what they do, when the snow really gets blowing on the road.'

'Aha! so that monstrosity has to stand idle too? And so how does it get out then?'

'Now, I didn't happen to ask.'

'Wouldn't they have to get men with shovels to help, just like other snowploughs? There, now we see it!'

'What?'

'That those machines don't really help when a spot gets really tight. Shall we go?'

'OK, let's go.'

And so they set off walking along the highway. Matti was still thinking as they walked about how it had to stop and wait too, even though it was supposed to go so fast that even the best trotting horses could not keep up. And why did Matti feel the need to almost poke fun at the railroad about not being able to get through the snow? If it had been a real miracle, then the snowdrifts would not be a problem – it would have gone over! And it would not have gone around rocks either. Moses was even able to make water run from a rock ... but he had the Spirit of the Lord within him.

As they walked along the main road, they began to see the buildings of Valkeiskylä at the end of the road.

'Whose cows are those?' Matti asked when he saw cows on the side of the road.

'Valkeiskylä cows,' Liisa said, but then she remembered something and said, 'Listen, Matti, I didn't remember to say what the pastor's wife told me when I visited in the winter.'

And Liisa said what the pastor's wife had told her, that the previous summer the railroad had run over a cow – and that the cow had split in half, with half of the carcass on either side of the road.

'Apparently it doesn't watch out ahead; it just runs at a full gallop, even if a person is in the way.'

'Do they have to be in the way?'

'Well, but a cow doesn't have the time to move ... or the brains.'

'No, but a person.'

'Even a person wouldn't have time to move ... apparently it doesn't look. Whoever happens to be in its way ... Apparently it whistles, and whoever doesn't ...'

'Does it whistle?'

'So I heard.'

'So it follows its same habits moving on land. If anyone gets run over, it's his own fault.'

'A person would have to be crazy to get run over when he could walk somewhere else just as well.'

'People should stay farther away.'

'Apparently sometimes it gets people from off to the side as well, if you don't stand back enough. I heard that one man who had gone too close was pulled along. It must have a pull that drags at you like rapids into a whirlpool.'

'And it takes you right along?'

'So they say.'

'A body could stand to keep farther off if he happened to get close to it someday – I could anyway.'

'I could too.'

Matti and Liisa walked on in perfect agreement that it was pure insanity – if they ever happened to get near it – to get in front of the railroad or even too close. Something like that you could watch from a little farther off just as well, from behind a fence, for example. It was not something to go touching. Who knew what something like that would do if you went teasing it?

It sure was a wild beast, it was, splitting a cow in two! And what poor person's cow had it been? And it would not stop even if it were about to run a person down! Matti and Liisa would not have been afraid for themselves, of course – if they ever happened to get near it – but there were also those who did not know what it does when you get close, and to them it would be dangerous.

At Valkeiskylä, Matti and Liisa walked even faster than elsewhere, not stopping at a single house, even though they were called insistently to many.

In the alderman's field, the master of the house was out harrowing. When he came to the corner of the fence, he stopped his horse and leaned against the fence to smoke. Matti and Liisa did not notice him there until they had already passed by.

'And where are you off to in such a hurry?' the alderman suddenly asked over the fence.

'Oh?' Matti and Liisa said at the same time, slightly startled.

'Where?' said Matti, 'off towards the church.'

'You're carrying quite a sack of food …'

'We have a little business there. We may have to stay there a bit past Sunday.'

'At the church?'

'Yes, at the church. And we do have some business on the far side of the church as well.'

'You aren't going to see the railroad, are you? Everyone is going there now. I just haven't had so much spare time.'

Matti turned the talk elsewhere.

'Is the harrowing going well?' he asked.

'Just like always. The dry fields are a little dusty … but I'm getting along.'

'We have to go,' Matti said, when they had stood and looked at each other for a little while.

'Don't you have time to stop in the house?'

'No, we don't really have time; we have to go. Good day then.'

'Good day,' the alderman said and was left smoking his pipe. Matti and Liisa set off walking, but they could feel in their backs that they were being watched … and that he was laughing at them to himself, the same as when he said that 'everyone is going there now.'

But Matti and Liisa did not say anything about this feeling

to each other.

They walked on, not meeting anyone, and soon the parsonage came into sight. It had already been midday when they departed from home – they had not managed to get away before then – and now the sun was already a way down. It was milking time, and smoke was rising straight into the air from the cow pen at every house. Liisa wondered if the person watching their home had already milked or if she was just starting the fire. Oh my, they hadn't said that the feed bucket was on the upper shelf in the granary ... but maybe she would still find it there. Liisa said this to Matti, and Matti also thought that surely she would find it there when she took down the milking pail.

Matti and Liisa came to a crossroads. One way, a shortcut, ran across the meadows straight through the parsonage yard to the church, but the other, the same main road by which they had come, went around the parsonage meadows and fields.

Matti stopped at the crossroads and waited for Liisa, who always walked a bit behind. Liisa sat down on the side of the road and began to put her shoes on – women always had a habit of putting their shoes on there, not presuming to walk through the parsonage yard unshod. But Matti wondered whether they should go through the meadows at all. Liisa thought that of course they should go through the meadows, since it was more direct.

But Matti replied that the gentlefolk at the parsonage would see them – they always sat on the front steps in the summer.

Liisa did not think it would matter even if they did see them – they had seen them before.

No, of course it would not matter, but still they might call them inside and ask where they were going and then who would explain to the pastor that they were going to the Lapinlahti church to hear a priest with greater gifts ... they might wonder whether their own parish priest was not good enough for them any more, even if they did not say so.

'Let's say we're on our way to see the railroad,' Liisa said.

Hmmm! Matti did not think they could really say that

either. And what if they did not manage to go to the railroad after all? Then they would be liars in the eyes of the pastor. Might they not instead return via the parsonage?

It was all the same to Liisa, whichever way they went, just so long as they went. But at least she still put her shoes on, since she had already started doing so.

And Matti and Liisa continued on along the main road. They circled the meadows and fields, walking past the parsonage veranda and approaching the church.

They sat down on the sacristy steps to rest. Matti set his knapsack down on a lower step, and Liisa began to remove her shoes.

But then suddenly from behind the sacristy along the main road came the whole household of the parsonage: the pastor, the pastor's wife, the young master and the young ladies, and then a few guests whom Matti and Liisa did not know. At first they did not notice that anyone was sitting on the stairs of the sacristy, going a little way past, but then the pastor's wife happened to turn her head. Matti lifted his hat, and Liisa stood up and curtsied. And now everyone stopped to chat.

'Good evening! Look, Matti and Liisa! Where are you going?' they were asked.

Liisa took the opportunity to speak.

'Good evening, Reverend Pastor – and to you, lady – hello! – we're coming from home – good evening, young misses – hello, hello! – we set off – look, it's the young master – I didn't even recognize you, since you've grown so big – hello! – we set off to walk a little, silly people that we are, before the hay cutting – Matti would have liked to stop at the house, but I said we didn't have time, but we meant to stop on the way back.'

'Is that so?' the pastor's wife said warmly, and the pastor inquired where they were off to.

'Just a little ways from here ... how far could it be, six miles and a little more – to the Lapinlahti road.'

'Are you off towards Lapinlahti?'

'Yes, in that direction. Matti has relations in a house there. Apparently you can even see the Lapinlahti church from its steps! They have always invited us to visit, although we've never gone before. And who are the gentlefolk's visitors?'

'Relatives of ours.'

'Have they come from very far?'

'From Helsinki. They came here on the railroad.'

'Oh, on the railroad?'

'Yes. And of course you, Matti and Liisa, will go and see the railroad since you are already off to Lapinlahti?'

'The railroad? I don't know ... there hasn't been any talk of it. Would we have time since we meant to make it back here to church by tomorrow?'

'You can always come to church. You should go, since you're already out. And couldn't you go to church in Lapinlahti?'

'Well ... well ... yes, of course, we aren't short on priests in our own parish either though.'

'Go, go see the railroad,' the pastor's wife urged them.

Liisa looked at Matti, but Matti did not say anything.

'Should we go ... who knows ... it certainly would be something to see.'

'And you should ride a little way on it too.'

'Oh, we don't have money to go riding on something like that; it will just be good that we can see it, old as we are.'

'It doesn't cost but half a normal coach fare – it's the same to travel on it as to take half a coach ride.'

'Is that so little? Nothing has ever been important enough for us to ride in a coach!'

But the pastor's wife did not abandon hope. She wanted absolutely for others to be able to enjoy the same fun that she had had.

'It will be worth the effort,' she said, 'and you will want to ride it too, once you see what it is. And then come to the parsonage on your way back.'

And the pastor's wife bade farewell to Matti and Liisa, following the others, who had already left.

When Liisa had removed her shoes and Matti had arranged his knapsack on his back, they continued their journey.

'What if we were to go, since they insisted so?' Liisa said.

'Yes, we really ought to go! What would we say to them later when they ask, if we didn't go now?'

This talk thrilled them both, Matti and Liisa, but neither said so to the other.

But Matti did feel like teasing a little.

'Liisa, why did you lie to the pastor's wife that we were going to see relatives?'

Liisa took the reproach seriously and replied, a little angrily. 'What should I have said? Would you have said something better?'

'Now don't now, don't now,' Matti said soothingly, 'it was good that you said something.'

And Liisa was appeased.

'You wouldn't have come up with even that – you just stood there, and couldn't get a single word out of your mouth.'

They were walking past the houses in the village, past fields and doorways. The main road ran through the fields and then, at the village gate, into the forest, and soon the houses and fields disappeared as they reached a bend the road.

It was unbroken forest nearly all the way to the village of Lapinlahti, just a meadow here and there, Matti and Liisa knew, and they hastened their pace in the cool of the evening. At times the road ran down into a dell, and then cold air would wash over the travellers from the marsh, but on harder ground the warm scent of forest heather always hung in the air. The dew had already fallen on the roadside grass, the evening was waning and night approaching, but they still did not see the cabin where they meant to rest. And without stopping and without speaking much one to the other, Matti and Liisa walked the hard cart tracks, one in each, Matti a little in front, Liisa attempting to keep up behind.

It was already mid-morning and the sun was shining down from a clear sky, warming the dirt and rocks of the highway on the steep slope of Isoharju Ridge. Sleep had tricked Matti and Liisa in their place of rest, keeping them lying in the dark sauna until full light. Would they still have time to make it to the railroad? Three miles still remained to the village of Lapinlahti, to the crossroads, from which it was goodness knew how far to the place where the railroad could be seen up close, but they had heard it could not be seen from the crossroads. Apparently they must arrive by midday if they wished to see it – that much they had learned at the cabin.

Matti and Liisa walked faster than normal, pressing up the hill. The heated dirt was burning Liisa's feet, and Matti's shoes were rubbing his heels. The sun scorched their necks almost as if it had been midday.

'Wait now, Matti. Not so fast. If only we had brought the horse. It wasn't needed for anything else.'

'What's wrong with walking? We're getting along. We've come this far.'

'Yes, of course ... although I don't imagine your heels are much in want of walking either.'

'Of course we have to walk; we won't get there by sitting.'

'But couldn't we sit and rest a little in any case; we haven't sat down since we left the cabin.'

'Are you tired?'

'If only I hadn't come at all!'

'Shall we turn back?'

'Let's go see it, since we've already set out to do so. But I won't go again. There is so much more of this hill – so far up – look, what is that there along the road?'

'Where? That's a rock.'

'No, beside the rock. A person! Isn't that Matliena?'

And indeed it was Liena the cupper sitting there beside the

rock on the other side of the highway ditch, smoking a short clay stub-pipe.

'Well, where has Matliena come from?'

'I'm coming from over Lapinlahti way. I was beginning to be so terribly tired from walking, so I sat down here to rest my feet. Do you think there is thunder in the air?'

'What business took you to Lapinlahti?'

'What else would take me so far but to see the railroad? Everyone else had already been there, and they don't speak of nothing else when I visit, so I had to go too. So much so that it began to be a shameful thing for a masseuse not to know herself what others were speaking of. I couldn't wait, so I set off on Saturday evening.'

'You went by foot?'

'A poor person like me has no horse – and the rich folk don't take me into their carriages. The master of the Huttula house left on the same day driving in this direction by himself, even though I purposely talked about my intentions in the sauna, where he could hear. Surely he could have taken another person in his carriage, someone who had cupped and massaged him so many times, but what do rich people care? He still has fresh marks from the cupping horns on his fat chins – just look if you happen to see him. Let that be the last time they get me into the sauna at that house – let them find a cupper somewhere else! And nary a house on the entire road,' Matliena sighed in conclusion.

'This is a lonely way – just a few cabins there along the road.'

'This is foolishness, this is, chasing after ghosts on a trek like this. An old person should believe things like that even without seeing – you are fools too for going!'

'We don't know if we're going yet. And what if we didn't?'

'Where are you going then?'

'We meant to go to Lapinlahti church.'

'Mean what you wish, but the railroad will draw you in – it drew me in.'

'And did you see it?'

'I did indeed.'

'And was it a fine thing? What was it like?'

'It was ... it was strange ... strange, strange ... I wouldn't have believed it.'

'It moved on wheels?'

'A great many wheels ... We stood there in front of the building – the one it drives in front of – and set in to wait.'

'What time does it come?'

'There isn't much time left until it comes – it comes at midday.'

'It's almost breakfast time already...'

'You'll have to walk quickly if you want to be there in time to see it.'

'We were meaning to go to church first and then go see it, if we happen to at all – surely it will wait for the church service before it leaves. It waited before.'

'It did?'

'When it was going on the water it waited on the shore through the whole church service.'

'Well, when it goes on land it doesn't seem to wait. First it comes up at quite a speed and then stands for a very short time before setting off again. In the middle of church.'

'I won't go to the railroad at all, Matti, if we have to go in the middle of church. You can go by yourself.'

'But when will you see it then?'

'What do I care if I see it at all, and my feet are aching so. I'm not going to go sinning over such a thing.'

'What sin is there in it?'

'What sin, eh? What is sin then, if that isn't, in the middle of church...'

Matti said nothing, even though Liisa expected that he would start arguing that what Liisa had called sin was not a sin at all.

'Is it very far past the church then?' Liisa had to ask when the others were not saying anything.

'It's still a good mile and a half from the crossroads.'*

'So far in this heat. If only there were a little breeze!'

'Where does the road split off that way?' Matti asked.

91

'It splits ... from here if you go a little way and go down the hill and climb to the top of another, then it splits off there on top of the hill. It goes off to the right hand and this road leads straight to the church. There is a red painted guidepost there that shows the way to go. You'll find it easily enough.'

And Matti and Liisa did indeed find the crossroads without searching – off it went to the right hand from the top of the hill, and the signs were as Matliena had said. From the crossroads, the church was visible a little lower down in the valley.

Liisa stopped to look at it, but Matti turned to the right without a second thought.

'So you are going there?' Liisa asked after Matti.

'Where else should I be going?'

'You can't during the service ... listen here ... wait!'

'It isn't even close to time for church yet. Come along if you're coming. We don't have time to dawdle.'

'Oh, Holy Father!'

But Matti just kept on going without pause – wicked man! – and Liisa had to follow after. There was nothing else for it, if she did not want them to be separated. How would they find each other again if one were to go here and the other there, in strange country like this? Perhaps they would be able to make it to church from there if they tried to be very quick.

'Wait, Matti. I'm coming – don't leave me!'

And so Liisa tried to keep up with Matti, quickly pounding the heated sand of the highway with her feet and every now and then gathering up the hems of her skirt. Before her walked Matti, rushing along, his blue homespun pants swinging on each leg in turn.

VI.

*T*he Lapinlahti railway station is built right into the forest. As you walk along the road that leads there, on one side there is dense forest and on the other stands a high ridge. The road runs along the ridge, but at the end of the ridge it loops around like the tip of a pine cone and there suddenly in front of you is the railroad and the station, before you even realize it.

First you see a red building, and then, as you continue turning around the tip of the cone, comes another red building with white trim and big double doors. But a little way off you see, first through the trees, and then in its entirety, the yellow clapboard station building with large windows and glass doors.

It still looked as if all at the station were asleep, partaking of the sweetest of morning slumber, since all the doors were still closed and the blinds down over the windows. All night they had stayed awake around the Midsummer bonfire atop the ridge. The 'masters of the railroad' had built it up there using their hired hands, and then all night they had drunk and shot their pistols into the side of a pine and yelled out huge, open-mouthed hurrahs at the sky. And when one keg of beer ran dry, they sent a man to fetch more from the village merchant. And this they offered to everyone – anyone who came was allowed to drink as he himself saw fit. The girls had had to drink as well – they were the only ones compelled – there was nothing for it – they did not wish to drink the gentlemen's drinks, but the book-keeper took them by the arms and threatened to pour it down their throats by force; but even he had not made it home on his own two feet – others had had to support him by the arm on either side. Even the inspector himself could be seen swaying as he descended the hill ... and it was already full daylight.

This is what the men sitting on the edge of the platform discussed as they looked along the straight rails as far as their eyes could see.

They were steady folk, the men from the village, who had slept their Midsummer night as peacefully as every other night, rising early in the morning as always, putting on their shoes, taking their watches from the hooks in their chambers and placing them under their waistbands, and then setting off walking towards the railroad. They had been there many times before, every Sunday, on no particular business, just to be there.

Other men sauntered along the track. They inspected the rails and the sleepers beneath them as they walked along without the slightest haste. They were the railroad workmen, and their beards had been shaved, leaving only a little fuzz beneath the jaw to curl against their collars. They knew when this or that rail had broken – a new one had had to be placed. This man or that man had been there setting it – How long will it last now? That one over there was looking rather worn already, but it might last for a while yet. How long? Half a year, perhaps a little more...

'However long it lasts, in the end we'll still have to pull it out of there; the bottom blocks already look like they're rotting,' said Ville, the previous winter's waterman at the Huttula house.

'It'll need new ones,' said another man a little way off.

'Looks that way,' said a third.

'The crown has plenty of those logs.'

'And when they run out, the men from the village will deliver more.'

They had come to the platform where the men from the village were still sitting, their legs dangling, smoking idly and spitting.

'Here's Ville strutting around like a gentlemen.'

'And why shouldn't I strut? Good morning! What's the good word?'

The men shook hands – the ones who were sitting on the edge of the platform and the ones who were walking along the track.

'So I shouldn't strut even when I have a road I built myself to walk along?'

'The crown's road, but made with our supplies,' said the farmers from the village.

'Your supplies?'

'The logs are ours. How would the crown build his roads if we didn't provide the materials?'

'There would always be someone to provide them.'

'Weren't you men at the bonfire last night?'

'I reckon all of us went to bed straight after bathing. The word is the gentlemen were drinking all last evening.'

'Drinking and making folks drink...'

'And that's why they're so up to sleeping now.'

'When are the gentlemen not up to that?'

'Even the station man is still resting.'

'Is he a gentleman too?'

'I'm sure he would like to think so.'

'He already has a star on his brow.'

'And yellow braids on his shoulders – after getting them he did nothing but walk back and forth in front of the glass doors and windows -- an amusing sight to watch.'

'A good man otherwise.'

'No complaints. He does his duty.'

'He'd drive you off the track, too, if he saw.'

'Not us – we have permission to walk where we wish – but you he would drive away.'

'And how would he do that?'

All of the men got up on the platform and set off walking unhurriedly across the rough gravel-surfaced yard towards the road.

They looked over the board fence at the postmistress's flower garden. The men wondered amongst themselves why anyone would grow flowers; what were they good for? Nothing – better to grow barley or peas. And then she stands around in that plot of hers and worries the ground with her shovel all the day long ... And she was so ill-tempered that she would rap on her window if someone leaned on the fence even a little, coming out into the yard and giving any poor wretch who tied his horse to it an earful of Swedish, even though a Finn could not get a word of her shouting and gibberish through his head. It would be the same if she didn't speak at all!

The men walked around the bend and continued along the road. One kicked a rock into the ditch with the toe of his boot.

'Someone looks like they're in a hurry – look out ahead.'

'I've never seen such an old man walking so fast.'

'His old lady's driving him.'

Here came Matti and Liisa ... Matti was a bit ahead, with Liisa trying to keep up behind. Matti was completely out of breath when he came up to the men.

'Where might you be rushing off to?' Ville asked, coming to a stop. The other men continued walking.

'He – here ... !' Matti gasped. 'Is that Ville? It is! Hel – lo!'

'So you've come to work on the railroad?'

'Not to wo – wo – ork. It's too ... too hot to be walking, it's ...'

'It is hot indeed. There looks to be thunder in the air.'

'Lo – oks ... that way. Is that the way ... we should go, Ville?'

'You're off to the station?'

'Is it still far?'

'It's just beyond that bend. You can already see it there.'

Liisa caught up to them. 'I told him not to hurry for nothing, but he didn't listen and wouldn't stop even though I was like to faint dead away!'

'You didn't faint!'

'Did I even have time to faint, with you charging on ahead like that? Has this man come from the railroad? Tell us, good sir!'

'Don't you recognize him? This is a man of our own parish. Last winter he was a lodger at the Huttula house.'

'Oh yes, Ville it is. In all this rush ... Won't you come with us and show us the way, Ville? In case we can't find it ourselves!'

Ville agreed.

'There isn't any rush, is there?' Matti asked, although he supposed there was.

There was no rush; Ville said the train would not come until about lunch time.

'So, the machine is coming?'

'Yes, yes, the machine – here they call it a train!'

'And us acting as if we were so short on time,' Liisa said and hurried, panting, alongside Ville to tell him how they thought they would not make it and how they had almost been running. 'Who could those men have been on the side of the road there back a ways? Were they drunk? It looked like it. We asked if it was leaving soon and they yelled, "It's already leaving! It's leaving! Run! You won't make it otherwise!" And us already rushing so – ohoh! – thinking we wouldn't make it after all.'

Matti had already let it go, but Liisa was still infuriated by having been forced to walk so fast just then.

'Is that it I can see over there?' Matti asked.

'Look, isn't that a red building! What is that pretty building for?'

'That's just a special building ... for the gentlemen. Peasant folk don't have any need for such a thing.' And Ville smiled ever so slightly. Liisa understood Ville and winked.

'They seem to need to have their special rooms here like everywhere else. I know all about it, having been a maidservant at the parsonage. I know ... but couldn't they have left off painting it? Look, Lord God Almighty, there's another, bigger one!'

'Let's keep going, and you'll see an even larger one than that. There, you can see it already.'

'Good L-lord! Look! It's ... it's even finer than the parsonage! Why would they build such a thing out here in the middle of the forest? Do gentlefolk live here?'

'Gentlefolk indeed, the masters of the railroad.'

'But where is it, the railroad?'

'Do you see that open place there, and those poles?'

'What poles are they?'

'There's a metal wire running along the top of them. Can you pick it out?'

'Look at that!'

'What is that open place?'

'Wait, Matti! And why have they cut an opening like that in the forest?'

'That's where the railroad runs, that is.'

'You don't say! That's where it goes? Lord Jesus bless us. And

there it is now! My goodness, how strange this feels!'

And tears came to Liisa's eyes.

Matti stopped to look as well. They had managed to cut it so straight – so straight it made his head spin.

Ville urged them on to take a closer look.

'Don't let's go,' Liisa pleaded and quickly sat down on the side of the road. 'Wait. I ... don't ... I don't dare go barefoot.'

'Let her stop and put on her shoes – let's go,' Matti said to Ville.

'Don't go now. Wait for me too, Ville dear.' Ville waited, and now Liisa thought Ville was the best man in the world. *I wouldn't even try to compare Matti to him – now there was a man for you – wouldn't wait for anyone if he was in a hurry himself.*

And Liisa tied her shoes in such a rush that beads of sweat broke out on her forehead.

'Come along now, and we'll have a closer look,' Ville said and took them across the yard to the front of the station building.

Liisa did not really know how she had come to stand before that building with its large windows and glass doors. Of course she had seen beautiful buildings and churches before, and the parsonage was a handsome building as well, but seeing those had never made her so ... but why did this feel so strange now? Why did it almost set her knees to shaking?

'This is where the inspector lives.'

'The inspector lives here? Here, in this big building?'

Doubt now crept into their minds, especially Matti's, but he was not able to express it. Ville must mean someone else – the foreman at the parsonage was called an inspector sometimes – but there must be other inspectors here. Such a fine house would not be given to a man like that. There must be someone more important living there.*

'Let's go to the other side of the building.'

Matti and Liisa walked around, following Ville, almost on tiptoe ... and neither of them could seem to breathe normally.

And now, wonder of wonders, on this side it was even more handsome than before.

Matti and Liisa did not rightly know what to look at – it was as if they were walking on a floor, and it was indeed a real floor, but why was there a floor out of doors? ... and windows made of two large pieces of glass ... and even more handsome doors ... writing on the walls ... and a bell fastened to the wall, a cord on the clapper ...

Ville took them to the other side of the platform where it sloped down next to the track. As they were walking by, Matti and Liisa caught a glimpse through one particular window of yellow wheels and heard a little tapping sound. At the edge of the roof, above the window, was something like a porcelain cup upside down, and from it came a metal wire that went to the top of a pole and from there to another and then again to another.

But Ville told Matti and Liisa to come and see the railroad.

Two narrow iron strips and blocks of wood set crosswise, side-by-side, perfectly straight as far as the eye could see – it made their heads spin to look at it – and in the other direction the same open space, narrowing gradually as it went.

'Is this it? Is this the railroad?' Liisa asked, her voice trembling slightly, and Matti joined in the same question with his eyes, his form of asking quavering as well.

'This is it; the train runs along these rails.'

'The machine?' asked Matti. 'Along these … logs?'

'Not the logs, the iron rails.'

'Along the rails … I don't quite understand … how does it do that? It moves on wheels?'

'Exactly.'

'Are they all the same size or … ?'

Didn't Matti know? Liisa could have told him that back during the winter.

'The front ones are larger, the engine's wheels, and the others are smaller,' Ville explained.

'So the front ones are larger? But now how do they … on those rails … I don't see how … won't they fall off?'

Aha, now! Even Liisa had not thought of that.

'They don't fall off,' Ville explained again. 'They're made in a way that … with grooves on both sides of the wheels so they can't slip.'

'Well now, then they wouldn't … But Matti still did not rightly understand how they stayed on without slipping. But surely they had arranged it so they would stay – they knew their business. Matti and Liisa touched the surface of the rails with their hands – it was so smooth.

'So this is the railroad,' Liisa said. 'And you, Matti, thinking the whole road was made of iron.'

'Did I think that?'

'You did, you did indeed. Don't you remember when you

were sitting on the bench in the cottage chopping tobacco and said that ...'

But Matti did not seem to be hearing Liisa.

'So that's it, so straight ... How far does it go like that?' he asked.

'Quite a ways. It just keeps going, just as flat.'

'Just as flat, you say?'

'Just as straight and flat. Sometimes it makes a turn, but it never goes up or down.'

'Is the land very flat here?'

'There are hills here just like everywhere else, but they go far around, and where they can't get around, they break a way for it to go through the hill.'

'Oh ho! Is that so?'

Matti had been pondering this the whole winter and had never figured it out, and as they were coming along the way, and especially near the hill, he had wondered how they would go downhill. Would not the carriages in the back overrun the ones in front? But now it would be easy to control, with a level path.

Liisa had a mind to try what it would be like for her to walk on it. A person on foot could surely walk on it, since it was as level as a bridge.

'May we walk on it?' she said, and put one of her feet on the track.

'There's a fine for anyone who walks on it,' Ville said.

'Dear God!' Liisa said in fright.

'Don't step on it. Can't you walk somewhere else?' Matti scolded.

'Does it get ruined if people walk on it?'

'That I don't know, but there is a strict ban on any outsider setting foot on it.'

'Did you have to put your foot on it?'

'All I did was touch it a little with one ... you won't fine me now, will you, Ville?' Liisa was beginning to be a little afraid that he might.

'It's neither here nor there to me. But if the inspector had happened to see from the window ...'

'Did he see?'

'Probably not. It looks like the drapes are still over the windows. They're likely still sleeping'.

'Whew, I was getting scared!'

'Why did you have to go and do that? If he had happened to see we would have had to pay a fine on top of all the rest,' Matti said, continuing his scolding.

Ville walked back up onto the platform, and Matti and Liisa hurried after.

The closer they came to the station building, the more handsome it looked, and the stranger things sounded the more they asked.

'Those wires up there on the roof, what are those for?'

Ville explained they were a sort of wire that one side was in Kajaani and the other in Kuopio, and that words moved along them from one end to the other.

'Words along a wire!'

'Yes, they move along it. You can hear the movement anytime if you go under the window to listen – you hear a clicking; he's in there clicking in that room over there right now, and the words are moving along the wire at this very moment.'

Matti and Liisa sneaked quietly under the window to listen. They didn't hear anything right then, but soon they started to hear a clicking.

'Now he's clicking. Are the words moving now?' they whispered to Ville.

'Yes, now.'

Matti began to cough.

'Quiet there! Look, now he's clearing his throat. Do you understand it, Ville, what he's clicking?' Liisa thought Ville was so wise that he should understand everything.

'No one understands it except those who have gone to the school,' Ville explained. 'Special men go to the school . . . we have one of those men here, too.'

'Goodness gracious! I'm sure I would never learn to understand no matter how long I listened, not any more than a woodpecker's tapping.'

Matti and Liisa listened next to the wall with their heads cocked until they no longer heard the clicking sound.

Then Ville called them over to look in through the glass door of the waiting hall.

Look, look, a clock ticking on the wall! What time is it? Matti and Liisa didn't know.

Ville looked at the hand of his own pocket watch and said it was in time with the railroad clock, that it was after nine, five minutes shy of the half.

'Buy a watch, Matti. You can get one cheap!'

Matti was startled, thinking, *does he want me to buy that one.* He started inspecting the notices on the door frame and the wall, and asked what was on them.

'Swedish,' Ville said.

'Is that so? Swedish? So that's why I can't understand a single word.'

Oh, so that's why? Liisa thought to say, but didn't. *Why should I go shaming him?*

'If they had been in Finnish it would have been nice to know what they've written on the walls.'

'There probably isn't anything special in them,' Ville said, sitting down on the steps.

'Probably not,' Matti said, sitting down next to him.

Liisa was still looking around and above, inspecting the clapboard walls, the decorated eaves, and the columns that held up the roof of the open porch.

But then she noticed the bell above her head.

It was like a dinner bell. Was it a dinner bell? No, it wasn't a dinner bell. Maybe they ring it when the railroad starts moving. Or maybe it rings when it leaves too? ... just like on the water, coming and going. Ville knew everything, no matter what they asked him.

'There's no dinner bell here then?' Matti asked.

It was not a dinner bell – there was no need for one, since each of the workmen had a watch in his pocket.

Matti was suddenly afraid that maybe he was going to try to

sell him his watch again and quickly turned the conversation elsewhere.

'Well now ... now I ... who did you say lives in this building, Ville?'

'The inspector lives here.'

'I don't imagine you mean a normal kind of inspector?'

'A gentleman he is, like all the others.'

'A real gentleman you say?'

'Well, what else? Of course he has to be a gentleman in a position like that.'

'Is that so ... well of course ... of course ...'

'Matti was probably thinking that it was the old foreman from our parsonage,' Liisa said.

'I did not. Never in the world would they take him here. I'm sure he was lying when he said he was coming. He probably never came, did he?'

'Yes, he's here as a station man.'

'That isn't a very high office, is it?'

'He thinks it is.'

'Well, of course, he would think so himself. He was like that at the parsonage too. He didn't have a very special job at all and thought he could treat the whole parish like we were fools. But he was wasting his time trying to play some for fools. Once he tried to convince me – and I'm sure he believed it himself – that the railroad carriages are drawn by horses just like other carriages, and that as they run they eat logs. That's what he said, just like that, only I knew what draws them and didn't say anything. I just let him believe what he wanted.'

'He is a little like that,' Ville agreed.

'And listen to this, Ville: once when Matti was at the parsonage he didn't give his horse anything, he didn't even tell him to take some hay, and Matti didn't have the nerve to ask, but when I visited later, the pastor's wife told him to put the horse in the stable and make mash for her from the house's own stores, and then he had to give it,' Liisa murmured to Ville, and then spoke even more quietly into Ville's ear: 'The maidservants said, and they would know, that whenever he went to the granary he put flour in his own sack and sold it. He might do that here too, so you shouldn't let him go alone to the flour storehouse.'

'He doesn't go to the flour storehouse here,' Ville said with a smile.

'Well, that's good, that's good.'

Matti and Ville sat down on the steps and started smoking from Matti's pouch. But Liisa could not bear to sit. She started walking around the station building. She sneaked about in the hot sun, her hands under her apron, looking in through the doors and windows, and when she could not see any other way, she got up on her tip-toes and stretched her neck. *Look at that window full of flowers, and there is a wall full of bright dishes – there are more there than on the wall of the parsonage, even though there are a lot there too. This must be a kitchen too.* There was no sign of anyone. It was strange that the maidservants got to sleep so late when it was already light out and time for breakfast.

'Eff-öö-arr ... För ...' Liisa spelled out from the door of the smaller red building in front of which she had ended up as she walked around. She had already circled and inspected all of the other buildings on that side of the yard many times. 'It must be Swedish ... emm-ää-enn-enn ... männ ...' Liisa was just about to get the word when she heard someone stepping lightly on the gravel behind her.

The person was rocking her head back and forth, humming and glancing down to each side of the hems of her skirt and then to the front and behind. Liisa thought she was very prettily dressed: a frock , ruffles, and a red scarf on her head. Perhaps she was the young lady of the house.

Liisa curtsied ... curtsied and wished her a good morning. But the other did not reply, did not even seem to notice. She walked past twirling something – was it a key? – on her forefinger, humming and glancing down at her sides, and every now and then jumped like a dance step.

'Didn't she see me? Or could she be so proud that she was pretending not to see?'

Liisa proceeded across the gravel yard to the other side, and when she saw the postmistress's flower garden, she went to look. The flowers growing there were gorgeous. What could their names be? Liisa knew one, the poppy. She had had that one growing herself behind the cottage, even though the blasted ram had jumped over the fence and eaten it ... and the pastor's wife herself had given her the seed and instructed her in how to plant it.

Liisa happened to lean against the flower garden fence – but then came a fierce rapping from the window. Liisa did not understand that the knocking was aimed at her and continued leaning against the fence. Then the window banged open and a shrill voice began to shout at Liisa.

'Not there, old woman, off! On your way with you!'

'Can't I just stand here? Will I ruin something by standing here?'

'Ruin it? ... of course you ruin it! ... why you asking then? ... won't you obey? ... go right now! ... I tell inspector ... whose hag you are? ... answer me!'

'I'm not anyone's hag – I'm a proper person!'

'Get away from there – don't touch fence. I say this last time!'

'I'm not touching it any more. Can't I even stand here?'

'Get away, old woman! You not able to be there and not touch. Go way, you look from far away if you want.'

'Well maybe I will go then.'

'Yes, yes! Why you come here at all?' and the windows slammed shut angrily.

'The people here! Yelling at folks and calling them old hags for no reason!' Liisa felt in her heart that she had suffered a clear injustice. What old hag? She was an honest man's wife, not some old hag. And what was going to be ruined even if she did lean against the fence a bit? She had been harassed for no reason, no reason at all.

In the meantime, Ville and Matti had been smoking and chatting on the stairs of the station building. When they saw Liisa approaching, Matti called her over.

'Liisa, come here a bit!'

Liisa came closer. 'Well, what's the matter?'

'Ville and I have been thinking over something a little together. What do you say about it?'

But Liisa had something of her own on her mind. 'People around here sure are strange. Even the gentlefolk in other places aren't like that. All you have to do is stand behind a fence, to say nothing of climbing over it, and there they are barking at you ... and calling you an old hag.'

'Let the dogs bark. Who was barking at you?'

'Some flapjaw!'

'Now listen here. I've been thinking about going on a little pleasure ride. What do you think?'

'What about me?'

'That was just what I was asking: do you want to go along?'

'On a pleasure ride?'

'Yeah, when the railroad machine comes here – it should come soon – we'll jump on board and ride a little way. Wouldn't it be nice to ride on it once in our lives? What do you say? Should we go?'

'What does it cost?'

'It doesn't cost much,' Ville explained. 'If you pay a mark you can ride a good while from here to the next station.'

'Yes, you see. A mark won't hurt much. And then we could say we've ridden on it. And it is why we came... .'

'What if we just see when it comes?'

'Then you won't have any time left to decide,' Ville explained again. 'You have to decide and pay ahead of time.'

'You have to pay the fare money ahead of time?'

'Yes, that's the rule here. Isn't it all the same when you pay? And you can be sure that it will take you all the way.'

'Yes, it's all the same. What do you think, Liisa?'

'Go ahead if you really want to.'

'I didn't want to so much, but I thought that if you did ... But if you don't, then...'

'Oh, let's go. But when will we be back?'

'You'll have plenty of time to get back this evening – just walk back along the track.'

'Are we allowed to walk on it?'

'Who would be there out in the woods to order you not to? Go right ahead. And it's a good road and won't lead you astray.'

Matti and Liisa both let out a good-natured laugh. Ville was such a tease ... so it won't lead us astray? Well, of course not!

'You could get back the same way you went if you waited a few hours,'Ville said.

But Matti and Liisa could walk the journey back well enough. It was good enough that they could ride there. Why would they do it twice?

And so Matti and Liisa had decided to go for a ride on the railroad. Matti immediately dug a mark out of his wallet and offered it to Ville so Ville could pay the fare. Ville said there was no hurry yet. The inspector who took the fare money was still asleep.

Would he wake up in time to take the money? That frightened Matti and Liisa a little – otherwise the waiting would have been fun.

But what sort of a ride would it be? It would probably go so fast that you could not look straight ahead. Would they even know what to do on it? But of course they would see what the others did.

Ville must know, since he had ridden it himself so many times. Yes, he was a good man, this Ville, telling them about everything and showing them around. Where would they have ended up in this strange land if Ville had not come along! Nothing at all would have come of their lives – nothing at all.

Midday was approaching, and the shades in the windows slowly began to rise. The doors began to open and shut; people came out of the building, yawning gentlemen and others.

That one has a handsome cap – that must be the inspector now! An entirely flat cap and the brim just so. Oh, so all the railroad gentlemen have them! That Ville, he knows everything and gives such good advice. But they all looked very proud – this one did not look to the side as he walked by either... .

Matti and Ville walked around the building and joined up with the same workmen and village farmers who had been walking along the road and then turned back when they met others who were headed for the station.

Liisa had gone into the inspector's kitchen to start eating from her bundle, since the day was so hot everywhere else that the butter would melt in one's hands. The same female Liisa had greeted outside was in the kitchen, and there were a few others as well. She must not be a real lady since she was lighting the fire in the stove. Liisa bade everyone good day again from the door, but did not receive a reply this time, either. She was looked at with narrowed eyes and asked what her business was. Liisa said she did not have any business – she had just come to wait. But to that she was told that this was not a place for waiting. 'Go to the waiting hall.'

'I couldn't go into the hall. The kitchen is good enough for me,' Liisa said humbly.

But now they laughed right to her face. Everyone in the kitchen laughed, and Liisa did not understand why they were laughing – but they seemed to be laughing at her. Liisa withdrew from the kitchen. She did not understand people here at all, either berating her or laughing at her, and everyone was so proud. The gentlefolk were not like this elsewhere.

Horses began arriving at the station, some drawing buggies, some drawing carts. A carriage hurtled in as well. Word had it that it was the crown bailiff's, who was coming with his wife on the railroad.

'What are you following me around for?' Matti hissed crossly under his breath into Liisa's ear.

You see, Matti could not countenance Liisa following him around when he was walking with the men. But where would Liisa have gone, not knowing anyone and with everyone so cross? Even the crown bailiff's driver had just bellowed down from his seat, 'Out of the way, woman!' – and Liisa had not been doing anything but standing a good ways off and looking at the horses and carriages.

A crowd had assembled in front of the larger of the red buildings, the one with the big double doors. Liisa went to see why they were standing there, and the men moved in that direction as well. *Now they're coming after me, not me after them*, thought Liisa.

In the big building, goods, trunks, and suitcases which were apparently going along on the journey were being weighed – so said Ville.

Matti pushed his way to the door frame and looked in at the man doing the weighing. He thought the man seemed familiar, and when he looked closer, it was the foreman! His jacket and hat were the same style as the train inspector's, although not as handsome. He was good at his job, measuring and lifting packages and writing in his book. He did not speak many words, and never once looked at the people at the door, although Matti waited for him to so he could greet him. Now and then he went with some papers to the main building. The crowd opened up before him, but even then he did not look at anyone.

Matti thought that when he came back, he would stand in front of the foreman so he would recognize him, but it never worked. Didn't the foreman know him any more? Or did he not want to see him?

After weighing the goods, the foreman lifted them onto a low wheeled cart and pushed them out the door. He pushed sternly, looking neither to one side nor the other, no matter who might fall beneath the cart. Matti nearly did himself, but even then the foreman did not notice him. Matti never would have thought the foreman could become such a mighty man.

'It will be coming soon,' Ville said, and this information put Matti and Liisa into a frenzy.

'Goodness me! You mean right now?'

'It will be here in half an hour. You should pay the fare now.'

'The fare, yes, well, how much was the fare again?'

'One mark.'

'Oh, a mark. What do you think? Shall we go, Liisa?'

'I don't know … what with all this rush. It is a mark … But why not go? I just don't know…'

'Go along now … you really have to go inside it too!'

'Won't you go with us, Ville?'

'Not me. You'll be just fine alone.'

'Yes, well, let's go then; let's go, since we've come this far.'

Matti dug the mark out of his pocket for Ville, and Ville went to buy the ticket.

And Matti and Liisa thought that now there was nothing for it and that soon they would have to go. They felt that some big event were approaching, something that had never happened before and might never come again. Not but this one time. And now it was coming, and that thought made their stomachs quiver and their voices tremble.

VII.

*M*atti and Liisa did not rightly know how they had ended up in the railway car. Liisa especially did not know.

And now they were in it!

And now it was setting off – the whole building, the doors and the windows and the floor ... Lord God Almighty, if only it would not fall apart!

Now they were in it, and now they were off. Liisa sat on the bench and held on tight. Matti stood between the benches, holding on as well.

The departure had come so suddenly, that they were not really aware of it until it had already happened. Matti and Liisa had waited for Ville to bring the ticket. Then the bell had rung with a clang above them, and Liisa had been more startled by it than she had ever been before. When she had recovered, there was the foreman, clanging the clapper.

But then they had heard a shrill whistle, and the people had called out: 'Here it comes! Here it comes!' And there it had come along the clearing, puffing and panting and snorting up to the platform. There had been such a fluttering in the pit of Liisa's stomach that she almost toppled over flat upon her back. And as it came it brought along rooms behind it that went along on wheels, with glass windows, and the rooms connected to each other, and itself it shone like gold and glittered so brightly that it was dazzling to the eyes. People had tumbled out, filling the platform.

And then Ville had come from the building, almost running,

taken them by the arm and pushed them in, giving them yellow paper tickets and telling them to show them when they were asked, and then he had gone on his way, leaving them there.

And then it had started to move, and now there they were in it, moving full tilt.

'Matti, come here. Sit down so you don't fall. There's room here next to me!' Liisa said in a trembling voice, squeezing the side of the bench as tightly as she could.

'There's nowhere, nowhere to fall,' Matti said, but he still moved over to sit on the bench and took hold of the handrail.

The speed continued to increase, the forest and land dashing by when they looked out the window. Occasionally it would whistle, sending a chill down their spines, and now and then white smoke would whip by outside the window.

Matti and Liisa sat opposite each other, staring at each other and just holding on. Both of them felt like they were sitting in a cart being drawn by a bolting horse, galloping down a hill without any reins. Once Liisa had shot some rapids, but that had not been as terrible as this. Liisa dared not look out the window; Matti only dared look out from time to time.

But Matti and Liisa nevertheless attempted to maintain appearances so neither could say the other had been afraid.

'There's nothing to be afraid of,' Liisa said, trying to sound convincing to Matti.

'Why should this be any stranger for us than for anyone else?'

'Are there other people here as well?'

Liisa was sitting with her back to the rest of the car and could not see anyone but Matti.

'You can see them right over there.'

Liisa calmed down a little, since there were others along as well.

'Are there many?'

'Can't you look yourself? Don't you dare turn your head?'

Liisa did. She let go with her hand and turned to look. Surely she could sit upright without holding on.

'What man is that there?'

'Where?'

'That one there, with the beard who is looking at us now.'

'Don't point! I don't know.'

'Matti, you don't have to hold on to the side of the bench. You can stay upright just as well without.'

'I'm not holding on because of that.'

'Why then?'

'No reason.'

Matti kept holding on for a little while – he did not want to stop holding on too quickly so Liisa would not think that he had been afraid of falling.

The conductor came and demanded their tickets. He had on a handsome uniform as well, with silver buttons, a star on his brow, and a leather case at his side. What did he carry in that? Liisa would have wanted to know, but he looked like such an important gentleman that she had not the nerve to ask.

'Sir, are you the captain?' she asked instead.

'I am the conductor.'

'Where is the captain?'

'Captain or conductor, it's all the same. Where is your ticket?'

'Matti, give them to him; you have them.'

Matti dug the tickets out of his pocket, and the conductor put them in his case.

'They're taken away?'

'Yes.'

'And there isn't going to be any kind of accident?'

'What accident?'

'Well, if it happened to fall. I mean, how else ... over a cow ... since it's going so fast...'

The conductor laughed and left the car.

'All the railroad gentlemen are so proud,' Liisa said to Matti, 'They don't answer questions even when you ask politely.'

'He wasn't proud – what were you doing going on about the cow – '

'Well, the pastor's wife said so!'

'I'm sure the conductor knows best.'

And Liisa let it be. He might know indeed. And there could not be any mortal danger here, since he had laughed.

And that laughter took away much of Matti and Liisa's fear.

They began to inspect the car: its walls, the ceiling, and benches, and looked more closely out the window.

The speed was still intense. The forest simply flashed and flashed on by. The message cord poles flew past as well, one after another, and when they happened upon a field or a meadow or a lake, they barely had time to see the scene before they were back in the forest again.

Not even the best trotting horse would be a match for this wild beast, Matti thought. But what was pulling it? This Matti could not comprehend.

He moved closer to the window. It was open.... *Wouldn't I be able to see from there, if I stuck my head out and looked at what was up in front doing the pulling?*

But Matti did not dare stick out his head. However, he tried to peep out the window from the side.

'Don't stick your head out there,' Liisa warned. 'Don't you remember what Ville warned us about?'

But for that very reason Matti now stuck his head out so that Liisa would not suppose that he did not dare. But the wind nearly tore the hat from his head, and Matti banged his cheek against the window frame.

'I can't see anything – it's going too fast to be able to see.'

'Now there you are! You almost dropped your cap,' Liisa said. But Matti did not respond. He simply sat silently.

Then suddenly the bearded man slipped over from the other bench to Matti and Liisa's bench and looked them both in the eye in turn, laughing in his eyes and at the corners of his mouth, but not out loud.

Liisa did not think he looked entirely in his right mind. The beard twitched about so strangely at the corners of his mouth, and he had on a large homespun coat with wide pockets. From the ripped corner of one pocket a bottle poked out askew.

Without saying a word, the man began to chuckle, glancing at each in turn, Matti and Liisa.

But at first both Matti and Liisa pretended he was not there.

'And where are m'lord and m'lady off to?' he asked after a

little while.

At hearing themselves referred to as a 'lord' and 'lady', Matti and Liisa deigned to look upon him.

'We aren't any old lords and ladies.'

'Oh, you aren't – he! he! he! – oh, I know who is a lord and

who is a lady!'

'Oh, you do! We're just taking a ride here.'

'Oh, you're just taking a ride ... just taking a ride ... he! he! hehe! hah! Oh, you're taking a ride – it must be fun to take a ride!'

'It seems you're having more fun than most,' Liisa said.

The man winked at Matti and nudged him with his elbow.

'More fun, eh, more fun? Ha! ha! he! hehe! M'lady saith that I am having more fun. What saith m'lord?'

Liisa was starting to be amused by the man's charming laugh. He noticed and laughed all the more heartily. Then he removed the bottle from his pocket.

'Doth m'lady know what I have here for m'lord? He! he! ha – ha – ho – ho!'

He spoke to Liisa and winked at Matti.

'How would we know? No one can see what someone else has in a bottle just by looking.'

'Oh, no one can see, no one can see! M'lady taunteth me, saying she cannot see. Let us drink, m'lord, and m'lady shall see!'

Matti did not touch the proffered bottle.

'Doth m'lord not dare drink on account of his lady?'

But now Matti did drink, just a little.

'Is m'lord not to drink as a man?'

Matti took a longer drink; however, as he drank, he looked along the length of the bottle at Liisa. Liisa looked a little offended, but not so much as Matti would have expected.

'Where do you hail from?' Matti now asked the stranger.

'From all around – ' (the stranger was taking a drink just then)' – from all around!'

'So you're one of those "men of the world".'

'Yes, one of those "men of the world" – he – he! He – he – he!'

'Where are you traveling?'

'Wherever, wherever, in the summer you can go wherever.'

'You must be a journeyman?'

'A journeyman I am, and in the summer I travel. Hi – hi – haha – ho! Another drink!'

Should he drink any more? Matti drank, but he did not dare look at Liisa.

'A cobbler or a tailor's journeyman?'

'A watchmaker's. Doth m'lord have a watch to be repaired?'

Matti acted as if he had not heard. He looked out the window and commented on their speed. It looked to Matti's eyes as if the speed was still increasing.

'It goes so fast that it makes a roaring in your ears.'

'He – he – he!' laughed the journeyman. '"Roaring in your

ears!" ... More?'

'Don't drink any more, Matti!' Liisa said severely.

'In honour of how fast we're going!' the journeyman said.

'In honour ... of how fast ... we're going ...' and after every word Matti took a drink.

* * * * *

'Toodledoo! It whistled! Toodledoo! Now we're moving!'

Matti had stood up, his hat knocked askew.

'Sit down, Matti, can you hear me? Oh you wicked man! You're drunk!'

'Be quiet, Liisa! I'm not drunk. Just let it go! Is it stopping?'

'Now it is stopping. Now we need to get off – we're going to be left in here!'

'M'lord should travel on one stop more!'

'Shut your mouth, you bum! You were the one who made him drink. Come along, Matti; can you see that all the others are already getting ready?'

'Shouldn't we ride one more stop, since we're already out – there's still daylight left!'

'No more!'

'We're setting off! Whee! There goes the whistle.'

'Oh, dear God!'

And the train moved off again, speeding up, soon moving at full clip once again.

Liisa sat, in turns lamenting and cursing Matti and the journeyman.

But the journeyman he-he-ed and ha-ha-ed and ho-ho-ed, and Matti revelled in the speed of their progress. The journeyman didn't think he had ever met up with such a funny man.

'He! he! he! Let the crown come race his stallions! He! he! he! Now we're galloping. Hey there mare! Liisa, oh, isn't this fun?'

'Oh, dear God!'

'M'lady should not be so distressed. Just allow m'lord his joyride!'

'Shut your mouth you, you bum, you scoundrel! Oh, oh, oh!'

'Don't fret, Liisa, don't fret; you're being pulled by the crown's stallion ... on horse, on horse, on horse!'

'Be quiet, Matti. Everyone is looking at you!'

'Let them look. Let them look! Judas take them!'

'And they're laughing at you.'

'Are they laughing?'

'Sit down and don't shout.'

Matti sat down and put his face in his hands. The conductor came to demand their tickets.

'We already gave them to you!'

'Those were for the last station – now you need new ones. Why didn't you get off at the last station?'

'Oh, dear sir, we would have gotten off, but I couldn't get my husband ...'

'Is he drunk?'

'No, no, he never has been before, and he isn't now; he's fallen sick; it must be the terrible speed that has gone to his head. He couldn't get out of his seat.'

'Speed to his head – he – he – he – The palsy took him!'

'A palsy? Surely not ... is that shameless pig still at it?'

'Don't call names!'

'I didn't, I didn't – but that man made him drink and wouldn't leave us alone. Oh, dear God!'

'You still have to pay for the ticket.'

'How much does it cost?'

'Two marks. It's a double charge.'

'Isn't the mark enough? I don't have.... . The one who tricked him into drinking should have to pay. Matti, give me your wallet. Do you hear?'

But Matti did not hear. He was already sleeping, resting on his hands. However, Liisa found the wallet and paid.

'Oh, bless my soul! What misfortunes we have had!'

But then the train whistled and stopped again. Liisa carried Matti out of the car with the help of the conductor and the journeyman. The journeyman he-he-ing and ho-ho-ing! Liisa moaned, and the conductor cursed.

'Don't curse him, dear sir. He isn't always like this. I don't know how this happened. The poor man hasn't drunk in many years; how could he hold it?' Liisa said to the conductor beseechingly.

But when the conductor had left them and reboarded the train, and the train had set off again, then Liisa dragged Matti away into the shelter of the buildings and there gave him such a smack upon the ear that she herself let out a cry herself.

It woke Matti up enough for him to ask, 'What was that?' And then, 'Whe – where are we?'

'Where can we be? It doesn't even look like our country. What world could this be?' and Liisa burst into tears again.

The land looked very strange – completely flat, without trees or forests other than far off in the distance.

'I'd like to sleep. Do you know where I could sleep?' Matti sputtered.

'Where would I put you to sleep now? Sleep where you are. There's a log for your head. Lie down on that pile of wood chips.'

Matti lay down on the chips at the base of the wood pile and immediately fell asleep.

Liisa sat down a few logs away.

Now their situation began to feel truly miserable to Liisa.

'Oh dear, if only we had never set out!' She had long been thinking this, since immediately after departing their yard, when Matti started to leave her behind, and then along the way, in the heat, and when they had to pass by the church. All this calamity was a punishment for that, and not unjustly. And in the commotion as they sped along, she was already thinking it … and then when Matti began to drink, she was already thinking that nothing good would ever come of this. And now there he sprawled! If only he would sober up so they could leave … But where would they go then? Would they even be able to find their way home? 'Oh, dear God!'

VIII.

*A*fternoon was already at hand, and Matti and Liisa were walking along the railroad, directing their slow progress at where they had just come from at the speed of fire.

Matti walked ahead, Liisa a bit behind, trying to keep up.

They did not speak to each other. Matti did not want to say anything, and Liisa did not dare. Liisa would still have liked to express her displeasure, and a desire to scold Matti still burned within her, but she did not dare let it loose.

After Matti had woken up, Liisa had set in on him, and her haranguing and berating had continued for some time, but when Matti had finally fully cleared his head, he had asked her to shut her mouth, asked once and then a second time politely, quietly, but when Liisa had only become more enraged, then Matti had said the third time, 'Quiet, woman, or no good will follow!' and at that Liisa had to give off quarrelling, although she was only able to restrain herself by great effort.

There was no sunshine in Matti's mood either when he awoke, looked around, and did not recognize their surroundings. He did not really remember what had happened, but neither did he ask.

He attempted to remember as he lugged his knapsack along upon his back, stepping from sleeper to sleeper without saying a word. He remembered a little, but not everything.

'I have your wallet,' Liisa said and thought that when he wanted it back then she would at least get to say, 'I certainly will not give it back. I don't think you're in any condition to be its bearer yet.'

But Matti did not want his wallet back. He walked as if he had not even heard. *He's ashamed*, thought Liisa.

'Two marks went completely to waste on this last leg of the journey. If only we had gotten off where we were supposed to at first, then that money wouldn't have been wasted.'

But this did not have any effect either.

And so they walked on again, silently along the arrow-straight track, and the going was miserable, very miserable for both – so much so that neither felt like chatting.

And even worse, the weather looked to be turning to rain. Clouds had been growing around the sun all day, and there had been rumbles of thunder at noon. But then the thunder had disappeared, and the wind had turned to the east, bringing rain.

Liisa had looked back a few times, but Matti not even once. She could not see the place they had set off walking from, but she could not make out anything in front either but the same straight, ever-narrowing clearing.

But suddenly both looked back. Their ears seemed to hear a whistling ...

And it was good they did look back. Both jumped as fast as could be, one to one side of the track, the other to the other, or they would have been run down.

It was the train, screeching angrily as it passed, careening between them. A blast of cold air licked at both their faces, and they could feel it all the way down to their spines.

There it goes, and here we are, thought Matti and Liisa. *And if things were fair, we would have been able to be in it now for those two marks, and we wouldn't have had to walk ... and there would have been change left over.* But neither expressed their thoughts to the other.

And then it began raining in earnest, immediately after the train had gone by, and it looked like it would not let up for many days. The rain rose from the east, and so would last. Liisa lifted her skirt over her head, and Matti raised the collar of his coat.

It was good that at least the railroad was staying dry. But otherwise nothing was good, just bad or miserable or worse. So they both felt. And they would have turned back ages ago if they had been going out, but since they were on their way home, they simply had to keep along. When would they arrive at their own cottage?

But they would never leave it again, not until the moon shone as bright as the sun in the middle of the day. There was no miracle so fantastic that they would go to have a look ... no, not if two such miracles were placed together and the peoples of all the world rushed to see.

And the rain only began to fall more heavily, and turned cold to boot. The clouds descended, the air turning grey as day approached its close.

No, they understood now that the railroads and other suchlike things had not been made for them – they were foolish and childish ever to have come. And if they had just not gone for a ride and had been content only to look on, then they would already have been almost at their home, but now when would they? The rain fell, pattering in the gloomy forest on either side of the track, and the wind blew hard, and the water ran in streams along the folds of their clothes, and through them. It blew past the brim of Matti's hat into his eyes and dripped through Liisa's wet skirt onto her neck.

It was still raining when Matti and Liisa arrived home, the

clouds still as low and the weather still as grey.

They were wet through, feet and pant legs and skirt hems covered in clay. How far had they travelled? They did not even know themselves. They had walked, lost, trudging through bogs and forests and trackless woods. At one place Matti had set out on a shortcut along a forest road, and Liisa had followed after without asking a word. But Matti had not gone far before the track began to fade. And Liisa had said nothing at this either, just following after and thinking, *Let him go where he will. Surely we will end up somewhere.*

They had finally met up with the highway by asking, had come to the snowplough, where their own road split off from the thoroughfare, and set off towards their cottage home.

And the magpie from the week before had started to cackle from his previous spot in the pine trees and jumped from tree to tree like a wet hooligan on either side of the road before the walkers.

There it is again, that same bird, Liisa had thought. *If we had guessed its laugh was an omen, this would not have happened.*

But neither Liisa nor Matti said anything, just thinking to themselves.

On the final stretch the feet of both began to slip – the clay beneath was slick – leaving long skid marks and often almost falling on their backs, but neither quite fell after all.

Bowed low was the rye in the field, and bowed low in places was the grass along the fence. Soaked black were the fences on their rainward sides, as were also the walls of the buildings and the sills of the windows.

And when they stepped in through the cottage porch, water was running through the roof, with a large pool upon the floor.

But the roof of the cottage itself had held, and the house sitter had warmed the stove, so they could dry their clothes.

She inquired eagerly about this and that, but when she received no answer, she stopped.

Matti and Liisa did not think, once they were in dry clothes, what other travellers would: *Now we've seen the world*; instead, they thought, *Things like that are not for us, and especially not railroads.*

And they never spoke a word of it, not to each other and not to anyone else. They turned to other subjects if they happened to approach it, and after being silent for a moment, started again from another place. And when they heard others speaking of the railroad, they moved away from the group or did not join in talk at all if they suspected the railroad might be spoken of.

* * *

But when they rose from their bed the next morning after arriving home and looked out the window, the sky in the east was already clear and fair weather was on its way.

Nothing so bad came of all of it – fair weather's come again, and now we can get to the hay.

So both Matti and Liisa thought, although, again, neither said ought of these thoughts to the other.

And when Liisa had gone to the pen to milk the cow, she heard the ringing of Matti sharpening his scythe.

'He's almost ready to mow. I should be off there soon myself.'

And Liisa suddenly felt such a cheerful feeling in her heart that tears came to her eyes, right there in the middle of milking.

The cloud bank moved ever higher as the morning passed, and its place was filled by a yellowish sky. On the damp grass in the yard the sun then began to glitter and raise steaming warmth from walls soaking with water.

Matti had now sharpened his scythe, and the grass on the wet verge was beginning to fall before it with a whispering sigh.

And Liisa had now milked her cow and strained the milk into the wooden tub and filled the cat's bowl on the corner of the hearth.

NOTES

22   In the original, the given name and surname are reversed, as in 'Korventausta's Matti' i.e. Matti of Korventausta. This convention is still not uncommon in Finland. In addition, throughout this dialogue and much of the novel, the characters frequently refer to each other in the third person, another convention that has not completely disappeared.

23   The explanation of why the foreman is called an inspector has been added for clarity.

24   The *tynnyri*, or 'barrel', a traditional unit of dry measurement, was equivalent to 32 kappa (the base unit of measurement) or 146.56 liters. Half a *tynnyri*, the volume referenced here, is almost exactly two imperial bushels. The *kappa* was equivalent to 4.58 liters.

27   This sentence does not occur in the original Finnish. In Finnish, the word for railroad is literally 'iron road' (*rautatie*, *rauta*=iron, *tie*=road), which is the basis for Matti's confusion.

29   One of the sources of conflict in Aleksis Kivi's *Seven Brothers* (1870), considered the first Finnish novel, is the requirement that young men learn to read before accepting confirmation.

30   * Slightly archaic Swedish: 'How much further is it to the railroad, Father?'
     ** Finland was an autonomous grand duchy within the Russian empire during this period, and thus ruled

by the tsars. However, many vestiges of life under the Swedish crown remained. The word for 'crown' here, *ruunu*, could also be translated as 'government'.

31 This sentence about the iron road, as well as the mention of the boardwalk in the previous sentence, do not occur in the original Finnish.

43 *A bundle of birch twigs traditionally used to beat oneself in the sauna to relax the muscles and facilitate exfoliation.
**The Plough, the Big Dipper.
***The Pleiades.

44 Orion.

46 These were most often straight, thin, shingle-like pieces of wood.

51 The traditional Finnish cottage had a formalized layout of hearth, windows, and benches around the outer walls. The word used for the women's side of the room here, *karsina*, literally refers to a small animal pen, but even when a cow was no longer kept within the living space, the word was still used to describe the section of the dwelling between the hearth and the wall opposite the door, where women would do their housework and tend the children.

52 Kekri, an ancient Finnish celebration marking the end of harvest season. Men dressed up as the 'Kekri Goats'; precursors of the Finnish Santa Claus, *Joulupukki*, (whose name literally means 'Yule Goat') would go from house to house begging for drinks.

55 Matti and Liisa live in a *savupirtti*, a 'smoke cottage', which lacks a chimney.

79 Another traditional unit of measurement, two *peninkulma*, each of which is 36,000 Swedish feet, 10,689 meters, or 6.6 miles.

91 'a good Swedish verst'. The *virsta*, or verst was normally 1/10 of a *peninkulma*, 3,600 feet, 1,067 meters, or two-thirds of a mile. However, a 'Swedish verst' was apparently longer, 2,672 meters, or about

1.6 miles. The differences in length of units with the same names are a result of the Swedish and Russian systems of measurement using a different base-unit length, although both were ostensibly one cubit.

99   Some material has been added here to make the reason for Matti's confusion more clear. The additions mimic those to the 1918 Estonian translation by Gustav Suits.

JONAS LIE

The Family at Gilje

(translated by Marie Wells)

Captain Jæger is the well-meaning but temperamental head of a rural family living in straitened circumstances in 1840s Norway. The novel focuses on the fates of the women of the family: the heroic Ma, who struggles unremittingly to keep up appearances and make ends meet, and their eldest daughter Thinka, forced to renounce the love of her life and marry an older and wealthier suitor. Then there is the younger daughter, the talented and beautiful Inger-Johanna, destined to make a splendid match – but will the captain with the brilliant diplomatic career ahead of him make her happy? With great empathy and affection for each member of the family Lie evokes the tragedy of hopes dashed by the harsh social and economic realities of the day, and the influence of one person who dares to think differently. Both in the landscape and in the characters the wildness of nature is played out against the constraints of culture.

ISBN 9781870041942
UK £14.95
(Paperback, 210 pages)

SVAVA JAKOBSDÓTTIR

Gunnlöth's Tale

(translated by Oliver Watts)

This spirited and at times sinister novel ensnares the reader in a tangled
encounter between modern-day Scandinavia and the ancient world of
myth. In the 1980s, a hardworking Icelandic businesswoman and her
teenage daughter Dís, who has been arrested for apparently committing
a strange and senseless robbery, are unwittingly drawn into a ritual-
bound world of goddesses, sacrificial priests, golden thrones, clashing
crags and kings-in-waiting. It is said that Gunnlöth was seduced by Odin
so he could win the 'mead' of poetry from her, but is that really true, and
why was Dís summoned to their world?

The boundaries dissolve and the parallels between Gunnlöth's circle
and the strange company into which Dís's mother is drawn as she fights
to clear Dís's name grow ever closer. The earth-cherishing goddess seems
set on a collision course with strategic thinker Odin who has discovered
that iron can be extracted from the marshes where she resides, and
environmental disaster also looms in the modern context, brought into
sharp focus by a shocking world event.

At the same time the novel is a moving, under-the-skin portrait of a
mother in crisis, cast into a maelstrom of conflicting emotions by seeing
her daughter under arrest and in prison. Dís's father has refused to get
involved, claiming he is too busy. Her mother is left to tussle with lawyers
and fight to clear Dís's name. She goes to Copenhagen in order to be near
the prison where Dís is on remand. The couple's business ambitions for a
government contract will be in shreds if the prosecution accuses Dís of
involvement with a terrorist group, but on the other hand, how can any
mother willingly pursue the option of agreeing that her own daughter is
mentally ill? Particularly when she has followed Dís into the depths of
legend in her quest for the truth?

ISBN 9781870041850
UK £9.95
(Paperback, 200 pages)

SELMA LAGERLÖF

Nils Holgersson's Wonderful Journey
(translated by Peter Graves)
Volume 1: ISBN 9781870041966
Volume 2: ISBN 9781870041973
UK £12.95 per volume
(Paperback)
Coming out in November 2012

Lord Arne's Silver
(translated by Sarah Death)
ISBN 9781870041904
UK £9.95
(Paperback)

The Phantom Carriage
(translated by Peter Graves)
ISBN 9781870041911
UK £11.95
(Paperback)

The Löwensköld Ring
(translated by Linda Schenk)
ISBN 9781870041928
UK £9.95
(Paperback)

Selma Lagerlöf (1858-1940) quickly established herself as a major author of novels and short stories, and her work has been translated into close to 50 languages. Most of the translations into English were made soon after the publication of the original Swedish texts and have long been out of date. 'Lagerlöf in English' provides English-language readers with high-quality new translations of a selection of the Nobel Laureate's most important texts.

Lightning Source UK Ltd.
Milton Keynes UK
UKOW030204140712

195980UK00003B/5/P